THE COVID CHRONICLES

A NOVEL

STU WHITNEY

To Lisa, Emily, and Elliot,
who make every day a story worth telling

ONE

I used to think prison letters were hard to read. They would arrive at my newspaper office with institutional markings and surprisingly fluid handwriting, full of back stories and rationalizations. For all their forced familiarity, there was an undertow of desperation, natural under the circumstances, and a misguided notion that reaching outside the walls with carefully worded pleas could make guilty men free. In my present condition, as a 53-year-old inmate at the South Dakota State Penitentiary in Sioux Falls, I know that prison letters are hard to write. Scratching words on lined paper, hoping someone takes them to heart, seems an inadequate way to explain how I went from respected journalist and devoted family man to convicted felon and shamed citizen, a sinking of fortunes uniquely suited to the soul-crushing year of 2020. My dedication to mask-wearing, the subject of dozens of self-important columns and fatherly lectures during the rise of the Covid pandemic in the Upper Midwest, has become as negligent as the guards will allow. The virus has raged through prison populations, and they tell us vaccines will be here soon, but I don't think much about it. The odds of finding contentment when I'm released are as unthinkable as the crime I committed, which resulted in the loss of a life, the ruination of my family and career and the realization that my words, once respected, are viewed as desolate overtures from the opposite side of the wall.

The penitentiary sits on a hill in the northern end of South Dakota's largest city, a former meatpacking town that has made strides to become part of the modern world. The fastest way for that to happen was to relax the state's usury laws in the 1980s, allowing banks to charge exorbitant interest rates to customers whose financial background was so bleak that they were desperate enough to accept such terms, and a credit card empire was born. Soon prominent banks were hanging a shingle in Sioux Falls, with some of their executives becoming billionaires by forming spin-off subprime lending ventures. That wealth seeped into other aspects of the community, which saw a pair of regional hospitals evolve into sprawling non-profit health systems with billions of dollars in revenue and a penchant for new construction. One of them took the name of a prominent credit card magnate in exchange for momentous donations, leaving little doubt that the city's thrust for relevance was tied to gouging unfortunate or reckless souls with interest rates as high as 79.9 percent on lines of credit they could not sustain, with no safety net in sight. In 1992, around the time I moved to town, a prominent national magazine ranked Sioux Falls as the best place to live in America.

The state prison owes its architecture to an era when Sioux Falls was part of the Dakota Territory and existed in the shadow of Yankton, the territorial capital. In 1876, a court in Yankton presided over the trial of Jack McCall, a 24-year-old drifter accused of ensuring "Wild Bill" Hickok's legend by shooting him in the back of the head during a poker game at Saloon No. 10 in Deadwood, on the edge of the Black Hills. Found guilty, McCall was sentenced by a federal judge to hang before a large and curious crowd of onlookers, becoming the first prisoner to face the death penalty in what is now South Dakota. Determined to get a piece of the action, Sioux Falls legislators lobbied to be the site of a new penitentiary. Their arguments proved persuasive, with a rising population and plenty of stone quarries offering proximity to building materials. Visible from the Big Sioux River, the prison opened in 1881 – eight years before South Dakota achieved statehood – with inmates shipped in from Detroit, many of whom worked in the quarry and spent their days hauling blocks of rocks for the wall that kept them enclosed.

I suppose there's irony in the fact that I hail from suburban Detroit and now find myself with the same vantage point as those early inmates, with less arduous prison labor. But they are not the ones I associate with this place. My mind instead drifts to Henry Eagle Bull, a member of the Oglala Lakota tribe from the Pine Ridge Reservation, brought to my attention at the Daily Gazette by a source who served as a prison counselor. She told me that Eagle Bull faced life without parole for manslaughter after beating a man to death during a drunken altercation in a reservation town when he was 24 years old. Four decades later, after letting his wild side subside with prodding from the warden, he was described by most at the prison as a model inmate, teaching classes on Lakota culture and artwork and organizing powwows on special weekends. After sending him a letter and getting on his guest list, I went up to the penitentiary on a summer morning, driving past pink quartzite walls and twisted barbed wire to the annex in which he was housed.

Eagle Bull wore a tan jumpsuit and sat with his knees raised at a child-sized desk in a room that seemed set up for our interview, with no other inmates around. He had strains of gray in his long black hair, and he gestured to some of his charcoal drawings on the table as a guard stood nearby. Not allowed a tape recorder, I scribbled notes on a sheet of paper the prison provided, a glimpse of my future literary endeavors. Eagle Bull told me in a quiet voice about his struggles growing up in the Pass Creek district of Pine Ridge, where the alcoholism rate hovers as high as 80 percent amid poverty and cultural erosion. He told me he studied art with his grandfather but learned drinking from his parents, particularly his mother, Lenora. Even when he moved to Wisconsin and became a common-law husband and father to three kids, working odd jobs to pay the bills, he found himself drawn back to the surroundings of Pine Ridge, where trouble was easy to find. Leading up to the evening in 1983 that sealed his fate, he drank all day and snorted heroin before meeting up with his mother at a bar near the reservation. They ended up at the home of a white rancher they both knew, asking for a drink of water and a few minutes of warmth on a chilly night. The rancher asked Lenora to stay and for Henry to leave, which led to a heated argument and, as Lenora later testified, a steady pummeling from Henry that left the old man dead on the floor.

When I looked up from my notetaking, Eagle Bull was regarding me carefully. He asked me what sort of article I planned to write, and I said something about wanting to tell his story as truthfully as possible. He then told me that he blacked out that night and didn't remember killing anyone. That was different from denying it happened. He said he remembered waking up the next morning in an abandoned car in the backyard of his grandmother's house, with blood on his clothes and dogs barking. He heard sirens in the distance, growing louder. He was assigned a public defender and agreed to plead guilty to first-degree manslaughter if prosecutors reduced charges against his mother, who had been at the scene of the crime. Lenora didn't display the same compassion for her son. She testified that she recalled seeing Henry punching and kicking the elderly rancher until he stopped moving, and that her son later tried unsuccessfully to set the house on fire.

When the judge sentenced him to life without parole, an unusually harsh penalty for manslaughter but permissible under South Dakota law, Eagle Bull looked back at his wife and children in the courtroom and saw them grow blurry and then vanish. "I knew that my life in the world that I once knew had ended," he told me. He continued to do drugs and pick fights in prison before finding a spiritual connection with some fellow inmates and turning the corner, using his artwork and experience to persuade others that daylight existed beyond those quartzite walls. Eagle Bull's own sense of hope wavered, even after I wrote a profile in the Gazette that raised the possibility his sentence could be commuted. He had lived in South Dakota long enough to understand the political implications for a Republican governor who showed leniency to an Indian who bludgeoned a white man, blackout or no blackout. He embraced spirituality but no longer believed in miracles. I received a few more letters from him over the years and heard from sources when he died. Tribal members held a gathering in Pine Ridge and recited a poem he had written as a message to fellow inmates: "Watch and wait for the full moon. Be inspired by great leaders. Let the rain and thunder teach you lessons. Study pictures. Be strong spiritually, emotionally, mentally and physically. Find a way out of prison every day."

Those words were meant for lifers, not me, but I use them as motivation. I want to tell my story, as anguished as it is, with the same clarity and conviction of Henry Eagle Bull, whether anyone reads it or not. The best time for writing is after returning from chow in the morning, when my cellmate, a domestic abuser who reserves his violence for women, goes back to sleep. The scrawl of my pencil irritated him at first, but he now says he finds it comforting, and wants to read what I write. I try to keep it from him, one of the last vestiges of privacy, but prison letters are meant to be read. They speak of pain and isolation and missed warnings, of moments where lives could have been lifted but instead teetered and splintered, their pieces a mere hint of the whole.

TWO

In a splendid spark of fate, the Daily Gazette building burned down in 1953. A press worker showed up to find flames surging from a storage room of the wood and brick structure in downtown Sioux Falls, where updates of faulty wiring had been put off until at least 1954. By the time firefighters gained control, the newsroom roof had collapsed and presses sat muted in pools of water. Eugene White, the paper's longtime publisher, received permission to walk through the debris to his office, where a framed picture of Mount Rushmore hung on one remaining wall. He made the decision to straighten it, giving him time to think. With telephone circuits and Associated Press services destroyed, not to mention historical archives, White knew that the hollowed-out Gazette would not be viewed as a respected chronicler of community events, but something to be pitied, at least temporarily. That would not do. He got word to his reporters that they should seize their notebooks and hit the streets, working sources to find enough stories to fill the next day's paper. He would take care of the rest.

He worked with the paper in Mitchell, an hour away, to secure use of their presses and acquired linotype equipment from local businesses. Teletype machines were shipped on cargo planes to restore the flow of AP bulletins. Temporary offices were set up at the Veteran of Foreign Wars building, where reporters banged out stories on typewriters on loan from a department store. White informed his circulation manager that bundles of comics were retrieved from the fire, allowing the Gazette to produce an eight-page newspaper for its 50,000 subscribers, mere hours after the blaze. Teenaged carriers, jostling for position, gathered behind the burned-out building as papers arrived from Mitchell bearing a banner headline: "WE ARE STILL HERE!" As editions were cycled through neighborhoods, cast onto stoops and stairwells, White resumed discussions about erecting a new Gazette building at the corner of one of the city's busiest intersections, a vision that became reality three years later. He hung his Mount Rushmore picture in a spacious corner office and reflected on how the fire had resulted in no injuries and accelerated the pace of progress, restoring public confidence in the company. Perhaps his decision to put off fixing the wiring had paid off. When he was asked to say a few words at the ribbon-cutting, White kept his comments brief. "The Daily Gazette serves as the eyes and ears of Sioux Falls while also reflecting the community's tremendous heart," he said. "I truly believe that this institution will last forever, no matter what plague or pestilence comes."

———————

I heard that story within minutes of arriving at the Daily Gazette as a recent college graduate and freshly hired sportswriter in the early 1990s. There was a plaque of White in the lobby that made his legacy hard to miss. Despite its outdated architecture and faded façade, the Gazette had maintained a place of prominence in a literal and figurative sense, with a circulation of 80,000 and a monopoly on local news apart from a pair of TV stations. Before the internet started pulling away classified advertising, foretelling the inevitable shift from print to digital news consumption, my early years at the paper were remnants of a golden age, with signs of the coming tsunami either underplayed or missed entirely. Walking into the place meant wading through a first floor filled with classified ad folks taking orders and, just down the hall, circulation managers barking at flustered reps. Retail advertising had its own wing upstairs, but the soul of the second floor was the newsroom, where reporters and editors embraced the bare-knuckled burden of gathering, prioritizing and presenting the daily report, upon which all the other departments depended.

The sports staff was headed by Joe Cummings, who was just a few years older than me and got the job after the departure of "Dakota" Don Aikens, a cranky local legend who covered high school and college events for 40 years before retiring and escaping to Arizona, rarely to be heard from again. The crew of reporters included Terry Finnegan, who matriculated at a private college in Minneapolis and regarded South Dakotans with anthropologic curiosity, connecting us as urban-bred outsiders on the graceless prairie. Our inexperienced sports staff was watched closely by executive editor Paul Huntsman, whose ascension to leadership, the story went, was owed more to machinations than merit. His preferred mode of communication was typewritten memos on Gazette stationery, informing us of various failings and signed at the bottom with a flourish. Cummings, anxious to prove his worth as a manager, hated the memos the most. He was a local product, a redheaded and muscle-bound native of Rapid City, what South Dakotans called a "West River" guy because he hailed from that side of the Missouri, America's longest river, which dissect the state. Cummings compensated for a lack of writing flair with computer literacy, understanding better than most that the industry's technological challenges were only beginning. Still, he was hard on himself and felt the sting of criticism, which we viewed more as a vulnerability than a weakness.

Our staff did predictions of high school and college football games each week, with success rates published in the paper. Knowing that Cummings was in last place and miserable about it, Terry got his hands on Gazette stationery and typed a note that looked like one of Huntsman's memos, instructing the sports editor to "come to my office to discuss your unsatisfactory football picks," followed by my best attempt at the swirled signature. The memo was prominent on Cummings' desk when he came in, and he took a second to digest the words before flinging the paper to the floor, exclaiming "I can't believe this shit!" and marching toward Huntsman's office. Terry and I looked at each other before arriving at an unspoken and ill-fated agreement that we would let the drama play out, which led to a three-day suspension for each of us and a newsroom lecture from Huntsman on the importance of respecting the authenticity of people's words and signatures.

Terry and I interpreted Cummings' lack of anger after that prank as a sign of maturity, bolstered by the fact that he kept the document as a souvenir. Even before that, we noted that he seemed old for his age. He was married and owned a house and made fun of our reliance on fast food, hauling in plates of home-prepared meals to devour with his protein shakes. "You guys need some direction," he'd tell us. "Maybe you should get married." A few weeks after we returned from suspension, he invited us out to a comedy club he frequented with his wife, Pam, whose chiseled features heralded her adherence to the same fitness regimen as her husband. Drinks flowed freely before the headliner came on, and Terry and I heckled the guy mercilessly when he confused Sioux Falls with neighboring Sioux City, a mistake he passed off as part of the act. "How does it feel to bomb in South Dakota?" shouted Terry, to which the sweat-drenched comedian responded with a string of profanities that sent older patrons to the exit.

The night began to spiral when we headed to the Lantern, a reliably run-down bar frequented by Gazette staffers. The fair-haired Pam, whose pale complexion reddened with drink, started running her hand over my jeans under the table when Cummings went to the bathroom. "What am I going to do with you?" she crooned into my ear, which I assumed was a rhetorical question but still foolishly replied, "I'll guess we'll find out!" When she showed up at my apartment later for a "nightcap" and explained that she had left Cummings passed out at home, I was dumbfounded enough to accept her advances, tasting tequila on her tongue as our bodies crashed to the couch. My torso twisted as she tugged roughly at my belt and growled, "I don't know about you, but

I just want to get fucked." We ended up on the floor before I came to my senses and disentangled myself with some effort, explaining that I could not have sex with my boss's wife and that she needed to leave. She cursed me with enough conviction that I feared she might harm me, but instead she gathered herself, mumbled something about picking the wrong ones every time, and stormed out the door.

I was in bed about an hour later when the banging started. It was Cummings. I had only heard him shout in anger a few times, around deadline on busy nights, but now his voice boomed through the hallway and into my bedroom, where I covered my head with a pillow. "Let me in, motherfucker!" he shouted while pounding on the door. I considered opening it and trying to level with him, explaining the drunken scenario, but my tussle with Pam made me fearful of any strength that might be greater than hers. So I lay there and didn't make a sound, and eventually the banging stopped. I heard him mutter a few final epithets before stumbling down the hallway and presumably home, where fresh recriminations awaited.

Life on the sports desk changed after that, with inside jokes and us-against-them attitudes replaced by firmly grasped grievance, suffered in silence. Terry left a few years later to take a job in Des Moines, and Cummings labored on without interference from Huntsman, who was dismissed when his flaws became evident to people whose opinions mattered. The new executive editor came from Missouri and shocked everyone by ensconcing himself at a standard-sized desk in the newsroom to communicate in real time. Raymond Ward was in his early 50s and, though cognizant of the shifting journalism landscape, set to the task of instilling stuff that mattered. Not long after he arrived, he called me over and explained that the Gazette had acquired data concerning South Dakota's governor and his use of state-owned aircraft. "This guy's a pilot and he loves to fly," he told me, waving his coffee mug around to illustrate his point. "According to sources, he's using these planes for personal trips with family members, and I want to nail him for it." When I reminded him that I worked in sports, he told me I was moving over to news temporarily to pursue the aircraft story along with our political reporter in Pierre, who was struggling to get the project moving.

"He's too close to the governor, if you ask me," Ward said. "I need a son of a bitch to tackle this thing. What do you think?" Cummings didn't put up a fight and tolerated my absence for a month, during which I discovered that the governor was logging flights as official business while traveling to family outings and sporting events, which the Gazette unveiled in a series that led to the tightening of state laws surrounding official travel and earned several national awards. There are few things newspaper executives enjoy more than winning contests, so it wasn't long before I was shifted to full-time news columnist, with Ward's orders non-specific but invigorating: "Raise hell and tell stories." Over the next few years, I built a following by wringing compelling narratives out of hard news, exploring the ways people were impacted by climactic events, adding layers to their lives.

When a construction company cut corners while renovating a downtown bakery, leading to the roof caving in and an upstairs loft collapsing, we heard on the scanner that a young woman was trapped, along with her dog. This was on a frigid day in December, raising concerns over whether she could survive. Bundled onlookers gathered across the street, straining to see firefighters picking through concrete and steel. Early in the afternoon they pulled out an appreciative Siberian Husky, and a few moments later the crowd cheered as the woman, a 22-year-old bar waitress, was lifted onto a stretcher, on her way to a full recovery and a measure of national renown. After a few days in the hospital during which she avoided media inquiries, I secured an interview through her personal injury lawyer, who wanted her story told.

We met at his office and he introduced me to Tiffany, a slender blonde who was polite but guarded, accompanied by her mother. She explained that she was still in bed on the late morning of the building collapse because she had been out with friends the night before. She was annoyed at the noise the workers made but also accustomed to it, so it was notable when the commotion became something different, like the tremor of an earthquake. Her dog, Luna, whimpered as the bed started sliding to the opposite corner of the room, picking up speed along the way. The crater opened and sent Tiffany tumbling to the first floor, where her mattress cushioned her fall and she lay in darkness, cold air roaming the wreckage.

She had unfurled her story with a detached tone, and she seemed surprised to hear my voice, reminding her that this was a conversation. "Were you scared?" I asked her, and rather than comment on the ridiculousness of the question, she seemed determined to articulate the condition of being in that moment, trapped and shivering. "Well, I had my phone, thank God," she said, nodding toward the iPhone on the conference table. "That is, I reached for it and was able to extend my hand just far enough to grab it and see if it would work. And I called my mom, because I figured whatever happened was bad enough that she was going to hear about it soon on the news. She answered the phone and kept asking, 'Where are you, honey? What's happening?' And I said, 'Mom, I'm in here. I'm underneath everything.'"

I glanced at her mother sitting near the wall, wiping her eyes. I later learned she had showed up at the scene screaming for them to get her daughter out, but the fire chief informed her that there was a chimney stack and other obstacles in the way, and they didn't want anything to topple further. Tiffany spoke in turns on the phone with her mother and the fire chief, trying to help pinpoint her location. It took three hours to get to Luna and a few more minutes to reach Tiffany, who saw the gloved hand of a rescue worker and held it tight. "He told me, 'We have you, and we're not going to let you go,'" she said. "Before I knew it, I was on a stretcher being checked out by medics as people cheered around me. It was all so bizarre, from lying in my bed in the morning to tumbling into this, like, abyss, where I didn't know if I would see my family again. I mean, how would you feel in that situation?"

I wasn't prepared for her to turn things around on me, and I stammered something about focusing on the big picture, a theme I later conveyed in my story. But in truth I was thinking about how fortunes can flicker at any moment, on a lazy morning, the bottom falling out, leaving fate in the hands of someone reaching through the rubble.

———

Changes at the Gazette came a few years later in a massive restructuring to counter plummeting ad revenue and an inability to sufficiently monetize the digital product, problems seen throughout the national chain. It was a "new beginning," we were told, which was not so much a lie as a euphemistic effort to soften the analysis that the industry was gravely wounded, forcing widespread layoffs. Online articles had been free for so long that most people weren't willing to pay, and digital competition was fierce. Print subscribers, many of them older, were pinched more and more, their rates raised to offset losses elsewhere. Our daily circulation was down to 10,000 and would keep sinking, with younger generations disinterested in the printed product, if they knew it existed at all.

Damage control came from a corporate vice president who visited Sioux Falls, wielding talking points of an "ever-changing media environment" that demanded "synergy targets" be identified. He told us that regional publishers, who had replaced local bosses to foster centralization, were being dismissed, and Raymond Ward was out as executive editor. This had apparently occurred overnight because Ward's desk was cleared off and we never got a chance to say goodbye. I reached out to him after the meeting, but he never responded, probably because I had taken his job through no knowledge of my own. The new organizational chart had me at the top as news director, with Joe Cummings and Gina Anderson, an education reporter who showed management material, listed as "content coaches." Our newsroom staff, which numbered more than 50 when I started, was down to 14. Any awkwardness over the fact that I was now Cummings' boss was eclipsed by the scope of our mission, working with a depleted staff that needed stable leadership and a sense of optimism, all while expanding their duties.

Sioux Falls wasn't going to stop growing and the Gazette wouldn't stop shrinking, so we needed everybody invested. I took a cue from our outgoing editor, eschewing a glassed-in office to set up shop in the newsroom. Cummings would supervise sports and business while Gina managed the news reporters and I handled Sunday centerpieces and watchdog projects. We covered an ice storm that blanketed the city one spring, tornadoes that blasted through a commercial district and a mayoral election that saw a former banker emerge victorious. We had talented young journalists who strived to make it hard for readers to live without us, and the days and weeks piled on top of each other.

Then one morning I walked into the building and took stock of the changes, which were gradual enough not to cause alarm but astounding when compared over time. That first floor that used to bustle with activity now consisted of desks and supplies abandoned in darkness, their functions long forgotten. The publisher's office was like a museum exhibit, not just the physical office but the job itself, once filled by powerful figures like Eugene White and now a cavernous void where I wandered in search of light. The newsroom at that point was more about engaged efficiency than the thrill of the chase. There were pods of reporters lost in earpieces, tapping away and occasionally noting something on social media that demanded attention. Gina was situated near the window, with Cummings in the center of the room, with our two remaining sports reporters and a lone photographer. He glanced over when I walked in and headed my way, typically a sign that there was breaking news.

It was March 10, 2020. We had been following the spread of the novel coronavirus that started in China before ravaging Europe and making its way to the United States, despite efforts to keep it contained. Our initial response as journalists, however misguided, was that it would have a similar impact as the Ebola virus or swine flu, a story to watch closely but not something that would affect the daily lives of most South Dakotans. But the virus was closing in, with basketball tournaments and other events canceled as health experts talked about "social distancing" as a way to "flatten the curve" and keep hospitals from being overwhelmed. Those developments were only partly on my mind during my nostalgic stroll, but Cummings' urgency drew my attention. He reached my desk and held up his phone to show me a headline he had just posted: "South Dakota confirms its first case of Covid-19."

THREE

Despite multiple attempts, Gina couldn't get the Zoom call to connect. The Gazette staff had been working from home for nearly a month, ever since that week in March when the virus became too immediate to ignore, and nerves were frayed. We had done remote work before and used Slack channels regularly, but major stories were best coordinated amid the concurrency of a newsroom, and we missed that human touch. Even the computer-savvy Cummings seemed flustered about having to set up an office in a corner of his basement typically reserved for weight training and leftover laundry, not the pursuit of ceaselessly significant news.

The number of Covid cases and deaths in South Dakota were rising at an alarming rate, making the state a "hot spot" amid America's patchwork response to a once-in-a-century pandemic. There were stories everywhere, from the state's lack of adequate testing to minimal stay-at-home restrictions and heartbreaking obituaries out of nursing homes, where the virus tore through communal conditions and at-risk residents. Much of the media focus was on Governor Kelly Lawton, a Republican firebrand who won the job two years earlier as part of a rapid rise through an increasingly divisive political landscape, not expecting a deadly contagion to stall her momentum. We had reached out as an editorial board to meet with the governor over Zoom, leading to a flurry of emails with her staff. Gina handled much of that correspondence and was now mortified that our screens didn't include a slot for Lawton and her recently hired policy director.

Cummings and I knew not to panic. While some Gazette staffers had wilted under the increased workload and personal upheaval of the previous month, Gina Anderson stood tall – quite literally. The 6-foot-2 former volleyball player once told me she was embarrassed by her lanky frame as a teenager, when any physical aberration was seen as a threat to be vanquished, with heckles in school hallways and names like "Gina the Giraffe." She had turned it around on them by embracing her genetic inheritance as a gift, displaying enough tenacity on the volleyball court to earn a scholarship to study journalism. As a young education reporter at the Gazette, she exposed financial misconduct within the upper ranks of a suburban school district, leading to the arrest and dismissal of the superintendent and finance officer. Now she was fretting over a call with the governor that would shed light on possibly the most significant public health crisis South Dakota had ever faced.

"I don't understand what's happening," Gina said, her annoyance visible on the screen. Cummings muttered a suggestion while multi-tasking on his end, a common occurrence during edit board. "The meeting isn't supposed to start for a few minutes," I offered, adding that it wouldn't be unprecedented for a politician to check in late. We were probably fortunate to be having the call at all, given the fractured relationship between Lawton and the Gazette. Like with so many other things that spring, the state of play had shifted. When the virus first reached South Dakota and it felt like we were all under siege, the governor had acted quickly, declaring a state of emergency, closing schools statewide and starting a series of daily briefings that delivered sobering projections about how many citizens could be infected. But as the weeks went on and other states issued stay-at-home orders and shuttered businesses to combat community spread, Lawton took an increasingly hands-off approach. She urged South Dakota residents to "make good decisions" and "wash your hands with soap and water," a mantra of personal responsibility that aligned with President Trump's downplaying of the crisis, a connection that critics saw as overly political in a time of public emergency.

Stories we did on Lawton at the time of her election revealed few hints that she would become a paragon of limited government at a time government was needed most. She grew up on a cattle ranch in western South Dakota, the daughter of an extension agent who served in the state legislature and took Kelly to Pierre occasionally, allowing her to sit at his desk in the House chamber and pretend to cast important votes. She was a college freshman at South Dakota State when 52 American hostages were released from Iranian captivity mere minutes after Ronald Reagan was sworn in as president in 1981, ending a period of American enfeeblement that she saw as a direct result of Jimmy Carter's failed leadership as a Democratic president. When her political science professor put a finer point on it, pointing to the energy crisis,

Soviet aggression and post-Watergate ripples that complicated the Carter presidency, Lawton tuned him out, as she would often tell reporters. "Even back then," she'd say, "I knew that some things in life were black and white." Though she said she respected George McGovern, the longtime South Dakota senator who ran for president in 1972, she viewed his landslide loss to Richard Nixon as a direct result of his weak stance on the Vietnam War and his coddling of those who protested it.

She kept a low profile during her time as a state legislator, marrying agricultural engineer Robby Lawton and staking a claim on a West River cattle ranch, ready to raise a family. Things started ratcheting up when she ran for U.S. House and knocked off the Democratic incumbent, mining the state GOP war chest and sweeping western and rural counties with her cowgirl bona fides. As part of the deal, she stayed in lockstep with establishment South Dakota Republicans as they tightened their electoral grip while blocking out reactionary elements of their party, a process known as "culling the crazies." Things shifted in 2016, however, when Trump stunned the world by commandeering the national ticket and winning the White House, a double-edged sword for mainstream GOPers distrustful of his character and political motives. While many of her colleagues held their nose at the thought of four years under Trump, Lawton extended her hand. She saw a portrait in strong governance, so much so that she spent time at the White House, meeting with the president and his family, and proclaimed her allegiance during a successful run for governor. It wasn't until the Covid crisis, though, that she made the transition from eager-to-please Trump loyalist to national conservative icon. Earlier in

2020 she had hired a new policy director, Norah Newcombe, who cut her teeth in far-right think tanks in Washington D.C. before heading to Pierre to "sharpen Governor Lawton's political profile and streamline her policy initiatives," according to a press release almost certainly written by Newcombe herself.

Lawton and her consultant made it clear they had ambitions well beyond the governorship, and there was much work to be done. As South Dakota's coronavirus response began to raise eyebrows, previously toothless messages from Lawton's Twitter account morphed into fiery edicts about the questionable science behind lockdowns and government overreach in states like California and New York, amplified by appearances on Fox News and other conservative outlets. When the Gazette published an editorial in April urging the governor to do more to protect her constituents as positive cases mounted, Newcombe sent me an email challenging our data and asking why we weren't dealing in good faith. "Editorials like these can affect the relationship you have with this office," she wrote. "Your tendency to attack the governor rather than stress the positive aspects of her leadership is a concern to us." It was not the sort of message one typically receives from political staffers, so it took a few minutes to sink in. My reply made it clear that we stood by our editorial but that we would give the governor every opportunity to share her perspective if we could schedule a time. Now we were set to get a "coronavirus update" from Lawton, and Gina appeared to have a breakthrough at just the right time. "OK, that link finally worked," she told us. "Here we go."

Lawton's presence on the screen revealed another of her political attributes – she was physically attractive, with high cheekbones and layered dark hair that could have been styled in Manhattan or Los Angeles or any of the other liberal enclaves she so readily disparaged. True to her ranch roots, though, her public appearances featured a bounty of jeans, snap shirts, horses and flags, playing to her characterization of South Dakota as a paradise of wide open spaces, where not even a potentially deadly virus could steal away one's freedom.

"I think it's important that we set some ground rules for this discussion," Newcombe said after we all introduced ourselves. "The governor has limited time and we don't want this going off on a bunch of different tangents."

I could see Gina reacting uncomfortably to that salvo, so I jumped in before she had a chance. "Well, Governor Lawton, we invited you here today to discuss your administration's response to the Covid crisis in South Dakota, so that will be the topic at hand. We'll be respectful of your time as we lay out some of the issues our readers are concerned about."

As discussed with Gina and Cummings ahead of time, I launched into a question about Lawton's decision not to provide statewide guidance on the closure of non-essential businesses such as restaurants, gyms, hair salons and retail stores. There were also no restrictions on indoor or outdoor gatherings beyond CDC recommendations. This placed the onus on municipalities to pass their own measures, leading to shifting safety provisions depending on where you traveled in South Dakota. Why not eliminate the confusion by establishing a coherent set of rules based on science and data for the entire state to follow?

"Well, I appreciate your question, but I believe we are listening to the science and data," Lawton responded. "Time and again during this situation I have placed my confidence in South Dakotans to do the right thing for themselves and their loved ones, knowing that lockdowns have had devastating effects for many Americans. If they don't feel comfortable going to the grocery store, they should not go. If they're sick, they should get tested or just stay home. We need to have respect for our neighbors rather than trying to fit everyone into a box based on an over-aggressive government. You never know when your own life might be affected."

Her expression didn't change much during her answer, so I waited a few moments to make sure she was finished before I followed up. "With all due respect, Governor, that's exactly what I'm talking about. People never know when they'll be affected, and they might not even know they have the disease. Asymptomatic carriers might be making what seems like a personal decision, but that decision is potentially endangering everyone they come across during their travels."

Newcombe jumped in at that point, which I figured might happen, saying that the governor's office has released studies about the prevalence of asymptomatic spread and that she would be happy to send along more documents on the subject.

"Are those the same documents that said it was a good idea to get South Dakota hospitals involved in clinical trials of hydroxychloroquine just because President Trump was pushing the drug?" I replied. We had intended to ask this later in the session, but the discussion had already gotten my blood boiling and I reached for the nearest quiver I could find.

"We're hopeful that the antimalarial drug can prove helpful as a therapeutic in the fight against the coronavirus," Lawton responded, maintaining her measured tone. "It's exciting to see South Dakota on the front lines of such a potentially historic effort."

Gina chimed in to cite studies that showed hydroxychloroquine to be ineffective in the treatment of hospitalized Covid patients and potentially harmful in some cases, which caused the governor to shake her head and sort through her notes while Newcombe went on the attack.

"I know we did introductions earlier but is this really it for your editorial board?" she asked. "Three people? Is that even a quorum? I realize this isn't the New York Times, but I'm a bit underwhelmed. It's interesting that some of your reporters point out that Gazette editorials don't reflect the entire newsroom – maybe some of those people should have their say."

Gina looked somewhat stunned on the screen. She had not signed up for this. "I'll tell you what, Norah," I said. "I'll make the decisions on how we handle our editorial board, and you focus on sending misleading press releases and badgering reporters."

Newcombe laughed at that, which lowered the temperature. But our point about South Dakota citizens seeking strong leadership when lives are at stake never sparked an enlightened discussion. Lawton had a different view of crisis management in the political realm and there was no room for middle ground, especially with her image being framed around limited government. The editorial board stayed on the call after the governor and Newcombe were gone, and Cummings had some thoughts on what had transpired. "Was that the best way to handle that?" he asked, to which I replied with reflective silence, emboldening him to continue. "I thought the objective was to maintain some level of professional relationship with the governor's office and not blow things up just to score some points over a Zoom call."

"What the hell are you talking about?" I shot back. "Who said I was looking to score points? People are dying, Joe. I'm not sure if you understand that, but that's what is happening, and we've got someone in charge who wants to do nothing and call herself a hero. That doesn't work for me, and it doesn't work for a lot of other people."

He responded that there were a lot of South Dakotans who shared Lawton's wariness of restrictions. "We don't always hear from them on social media, but they're out there," he pointed out. Either way, he said, presenting rational arguments was the best way to be viewed as a leading voice on the issue, rather than engaging in petty squabbles. "People are counting on us to provide reliable information and tell personal stories about the pandemic," Cummings said. "If we ever lose sight of that, we could be in trouble."

"And Norah Newcombe will be in trouble if she continues to insult our newspaper to my face," I countered. "But you're right about the other stuff. Those stories need to be told."

———————

Gina came up with the idea to begin a series of profiles on people whose lives had been dramatically altered by the pandemic in South Dakota, a recognition that numbers alone couldn't illustrate the toll of the virus. We called them the "Covid Chronicles," and I volunteered to write the first installment to establish what we were trying to do. That's how I found myself on the phone with a man named Robert

Christensen, whose wife was one of the earliest South Dakota coronavirus fatalities. He was from a neighboring community and familiar with my writing, so we exchanged pleasantries before I asked about his wife, Linda, who was 53 and a mother to three college-aged children when she died. When the kids were a bit younger, Robert said, she volunteered at their school as musical director, helping put on plays and musicals, including a rousing production of "Beauty and the Beast" that featured her daughter as Belle, with hand-sewn costumes by Linda and standing ovations over the course of several nights. "My daughter handed Linda a rose on stage the final night, as people clapped and cheered, and we might as well have been on Broadway," said Robert, who ran an insurance agency. "I never saw Linda more happy." When the kids left for college, she stayed busy by giving piano lessons from her home, allowing families to pay as they could. Every December she would use the community center for a holiday recital, with the children getting dressed up to play Christmas songs for their families with apple cider and cookies and decorations. "She didn't want just a normal recital," her husband told me. "She wanted it to be special for the families."

He was pretty sure she contracted the virus from her aunt and uncle, who lived nearby and later tested positive. Linda had mentioned not feeling well on a Saturday morning, but she did housework and made sandwiches for lunch before complaining of heartburn and laying down for a nap. At around 3 p.m., she told her husband she was having trouble breathing and needed to go to the hospital. He helped her into her slippers and got her into the car, calling ahead to warn them of possible coronavirus exposure. "Two nurses met us outside the ER wearing what looked like space suits,"

Robert told me. "One of them mentioned that Linda's lips were turning blue, and they rushed her inside and told me to go back home. No family members were allowed. From what I understand, they put her on a ventilator." When I asked Robert how long his wife was in the hospital, I heard his throat catch. "She died three hours after I dropped her off," he said.

There was a private family gathering at the gravesite, a far cry from the funeral that Richard said he would have given her, and he recalled the pastor leading them in prayer: "God is our refuge and strength, close at hand in our distress; meet us in our sorrow and lift our eyes to the peace and light of your constant care." He told me the words rang hollow, for the first time in his life, because his wife devoted her life to serving others and died a sudden, undignified death that didn't allow her good deeds and graces to be celebrated. She was making sandwiches in the kitchen one minute and a few hours later she was gasping for breath, and then gone, with no family at her bedside to assuage her fears. "I fail to see any refuge or strength in a world where that can take place," Robert told me. "This virus can go to hell, as far as I'm concerned."

His own Covid battle, exacerbated by obesity and previous heart problems, necessitated a trip to the hospital a week after his wife's funeral. Clots developed in his legs and torso, and doctors briefly considered amputation. "They cut open my calves on both sides and just below my belly from hip to hip," he said. "They removed a four-inch clot from my aorta. The vascular doc basically called me a living miracle." He recalled waking up in the hospital, scared and disoriented, looking down at his legs to make sure they were still there. It almost seemed selfish to be worried about keeping his own body intact after his family had been torn apart, he told me. After a few days, the incisions healed and he was permitted to go home, where his kids were taking college classes online and had prepared for their father's return. It took all three of them to perform the domestic duties that would have been handled by their mother, but they made him as comfortable as possible and considered themselves blessed to have him around.

"That doesn't mean they didn't miss their mother," Robert said. "Far from it. Everything we did offered reminders she was gone, to the point where escaping our grief became impossible, so we didn't try to hide it. We talked about Linda's tater-tot hot dish, her strategies in Scrabble, what movies she liked to watch. We realized that every aspect of our lives was tied to her kindness and character, and we weren't ready for it to be over, though we had no say in it whatsoever. Her absence is now the largest presence in our lives."

I was struck by that quote and used it prominently in my story, which ran as a Sunday centerpiece kicking off our series. We sent a photographer to get images of the family outside their home, masked up and gathered on the front porch, Robert surrounded by his son and two daughters, staring into the camera, likely relieved that no one expected them to smile.

FOUR

The football workout was in full swing when I arrived – six Edison High kids executing pass plays on an overgrown field behind the Methodist church. There weren't many houses adjacent to the field and the church blocked the view from the other side, making it a secluded spot. That was by design on a Saturday afternoon in mid-May, with classes still online and off-campus gatherings discouraged. My son, Nathan, had been asked to show up at an informal practice without coaches, just a group of skill players looking to develop chemistry and stay sharp as they prepared for the fall season. After turning down Nate's requests to hang out with friends during the first two months of the pandemic, fearful of him being infected and bringing it home, I relented when I heard about the workout. This was a good opportunity for him.

He hadn't played tackle football since third grade but was viewed, from what he'd told me, as someone who could help Edison win games as a wide receiver in 2020. He started getting Snapchat messages from some of the older players after taking a throwaway class called Team Sports, where he showed his ability to shake defenders and make tough catches during a unit on flag football. It took only a few minutes standing in the church lot for me to see him snag a pass over the middle, reaching out with one gloved hand to haul it in. That drew a howl of approval from quarterback Brad Hawkins, whose muscle shirt revealed the upper-body strength that helped make him a college prospect approaching his senior year if academics didn't get in the way. Hawkins was a bit of a live wire, my son informed me, frequently in trouble at school and eager to organize parties if someone else provided the location and the beer, pandemic or no pandemic. His sturdy frame and ability to throw a football 50 yards in the air glossed over some of that behavior, but Nate had tried to keep his distance. Now that was becoming difficult, because Hawkins and running back Tommy Burgess were looking for talent. The Nighthawks lost in the state quarterfinals in 2019, their junior year, and the entire offensive line was expected back in the fall, not to mention a stingy defense. They were thin at receiver, though, and saw Nate, one grade younger, as a possible solution.

"You must have gotten a VIP pass!" came a booming voice behind me, causing some of the players to glance over. A towering figure in a tattered sweatshirt was approaching, solidly built with graying goatee and a bit of a limp. He seemed intent on shaking my hand until my body language made it clear that I wanted to keep some distance. "Oh, shit, I almost forgot! Six feet, right...and no shaking hands! So many rules to remember!" He was chuckling slightly and throwing up his hands in mock surrender. "Cap Hawkins, by the way. Brad's old man. You're not going to get these boys in trouble for running a workout, are you? Write an article in the paper?" I told him no, pointing out that my son was one of the participants. "I heard he has some pretty good hands, decent speed," he replied, surveying the field like a scout. "We're going to need a little bit of that to get to the finals this year. These boys deserve a chance to shine after everything that's happened."

I had forgotten that his son also starred on the Edison basketball team, which was top-ranked heading into the state tournament when the coronavirus hit South Dakota and everything was canceled. The girls tournaments had already started when the activities association pulled the plug and players were called off the floor during warmups, with the boys scrapped the following week. "All that work the boys put in to reach that point, and it's just gone. Like snapping your fingers," Cap said. "Brad went down in his room and just started pounding the walls when he found out, and I let him do it. Had to get that anger out. Can't let it bubble up inside. I told him, 'At least you're not a senior, son. You've still got another year left.' Those seniors got screwed something fierce, all because of some virus that even the experts said was no big deal at the start. Then dominoes started falling. Science. If you ask me, this whole 'rona thing ain't nothing worse than the flu, except a few more old people dying. It don't affect these boys. Imagine not being able to play in the state tournament as a senior, not being able to go to prom and fool around in the parking lot with your girlfriend or whatever. What do you call those, rites of passage? All gone because some liberal politicians are desperate to control people and keep Trump from being re-elected." I turned to respond, and he started laughing again, a raspy-sounding reflex. "I'm just jerking your chain, man! I know that newspaper of yours has a different view. But we're going to make sure nothing happens to fuck up a perfectly good football season this fall — I can tell you that. Did you play in high school?" I told him I was more into hockey, which led to a pause in the conversation as we watched Brad show one of the receivers how to run a route. "When I was in high school, if you didn't play football, you were a pussy," Cap finally said, staring straight at the field and not laughing this time. "Maybe it was different in Michigan."

I had written about my background in the Gazette, so it didn't surprise me that he knew my home state. But his tone hinted at vulnerabilities I rarely addressed, even to myself, pertaining to my father and a childhood that unfolded far from South Dakota and the likes of Cap Hawkins. My first sports-related memory involving my dad was when he coached my older brother's Little League baseball team. We had moved out of our home in Southfield after my dad was promoted at his advertising firm, which handled accounts for Detroit automakers. I was about to enter first grade when we relocated to Grosse Pointe, a collection of five suburban boroughs east of Detroit on the banks of Lake St. Clair. The ritziest of the enclaves was Grosse Pointe Shores, where Henry Ford's son, Edsel, built his mansion during the auto boom as a buffer to the burgeoning Motor City, presaging a racial divide between suburbs and inner city that in many ways defined Detroit's fortunes.

We settled for a brick colonial in Grosse Pointe Park, close enough to the water that my brother, Wayne, and I could hear horns of freighters churning toward the Detroit River from our bedrooms. Early summer evenings were for baseball, with my dad coaching Wayne's team, the Braves. Of all the games I attended, darting around to collect foul balls, the only on-field action I recall distinctly is the play that ended it all. My dad was coaching third base and Wayne was on first when one of the Braves belted a ball into the outfield, putting my brother in motion. My dad windmilled his arm as Wayne, skidding on the infield dirt, rounded second, trying to beat the throw. He was tagged forcibly in mid-slide and lay in a swirl of dust, the third baseman adding to his shame by declaring "You're out!" to echo the umpire's verdict. That incensed my dad, who grabbed the kid roughly by his jersey and shouted, "No, you're out!" as parents in the grandstand gasped. The ensuing fracas, compounded by the kid's parents threatening to call the cops, resulted in my dad getting permanently banned from the league, a less-than-ideal way to weave our family into the community fabric, as my mom angrily asserted when the decision came down. I remember my dad writing a letter to the league pleading for leniency, talking about his special connection to the rapidly improving Braves, an appeal that even at my age seemed overwrought and was soundly rejected.

That must have soured him on "mainstream" sports, because soon Wayne and I were being introduced to the wonders of youth hockey. My dad regaled us with stories of the legendary Gordie Howe and flooded our backyard to create a rough-edged ice rink, where we skated until being called in for dinner. I took the sport more seriously than Wayne and ended up on the travel team in Grosse Pointe, separating me from school friends who focused on football and basketball. But my father and I were spending a lot of time together, driving to games and practices and making trips to Olympia Stadium to cheer on the Red Wings. My dad never played hockey but told me about his days serving as student manager for the lacrosse team at Cornell, a sport that used "a lot of the same positioning," as he put it. When my first season ended, there was a postseason banquet at the country club, where I was lauded as top scorer. My dad flashed me a grin that claimed justification for uprooting my athletic existence, and I sat there in my cuffed-up khakis, taking note of what it felt like to make my father proud.

It was a feeling I pursued throughout my childhood, with sporadic success. About a year after moving to our house on Lakepointe Street, I started a late-afternoon ritual of walking four blocks to the corner of Jefferson Avenue, which connected Grosse Pointe and Detroit, to wait for my dad to come home from work. He would pull over and open the passenger door of his silver Cutlass, smiling and saying, "Need a lift?" as I scrambled into position for the short ride home. Our conversations were short and light, and he'd comment on my strength as I carried in his briefcase. The toughest days were Friday, when sometimes I stood there for as long as an hour and the Cutlass never materialized, forcing me to determine the appropriate moment in my mind to surrender hope and start walking home. "Maybe he had to work late," my mom would say unconvincingly. It occurred to me later that my journeys to Jefferson Avenue were in reaction to clues – a late-night door slam or sarcastic laugh – that my parents' marriage was in jeopardy, making me want to ensure my father returned home. Other warning signs were less subtle, such as finding my mom sitting on the floor of the basement laundry room, smoking a cigarette, normally tidy light-brown hair in disrepair. That fact that she was smoking, which I had never seen her do, was less jarring than the fact that she made no attempt to conceal it while peering up at me, puffy-eyed, from the concrete floor. "Go upstairs," she managed to say. "Everything's fine."

My desire to believe her, coupled with the fear of the alternative, was strong enough that I didn't tell Wayne about what I saw. I convinced myself that mothers were sometimes sad for no reason and then magically found their footing, waving away the previous malaise. The childishness of that notion became apparent soon after, when my parents sat us down in the living room and explained that they had some things to figure out and would be separating, though it had nothing to do with how much they loved us or anything that we did. "We're still a family," insisted my dad, who took Wayne and me about a month later to where he was living with his girlfriend, a petite brunette with a pinball machine in her garage and a husband in her rear-view mirror. My brother and I played pinball and ate pizza until it was time to go, and Dad drove us home, explaining on the way that he and our mother would not be reconciling but that he would still be a part of our lives. "You mean like what we just did, or actual lives?" Wayne said from the passenger seat as I sniffled in the back. "That's a ridiculous question," answered my father, who hadn't answered it by the time he pulled into the driveway and dropped us off.

My mother, who had majored in literature and garnered most of her practical experience from taking care of her family, started attending night school to earn a degree in bookkeeping, her most direct acknowledgement that our lives had been irrevocably altered. Money, something my brother and I had rarely heard discussed as a household matter, became a frequent topic of conversation, usually in her phone conversations with our father but also occasionally with us. This emphasis on frugality was problematic growing up in Grosse Pointe, where not owning the proper brand of jeans or top siders could lead to social estrangement, but it didn't seem to bother Wayne. He was an honor student who played the clarinet, entered math competitions, and showed open disdain for "preppies" in pink Polos. Rather than dwell on the past, he encouraged Mom to get out of her funk and host a local singles group, which resulted in wine stains on the carpet and a date with a local restaurant owner, who spent most of the night, our mother told us, prattling on about his ex-wife.

My reaction to the divorce was more hostile. I started hanging around with the Vicker brothers, a trio of miscreants who lived down the street and were viewed by most parents as problems to avoid, especially after one of their babysitters spent time in the hospital and had to move out of state, as legend had it. It started with Ricky, the oldest and most degenerate, clumsily tossing a Frisbee at me as I walked past their house and expressing amazement at my ability to throw it behind my back. He demanded I show him the trick, but he gave up after a few attempts, asking if I had any money. We started riding our bikes, along with his brothers, down to the market to buy candy, with the Vickers accosting kids we encountered and turning on me when no one else was around. "Do you know what a pussy is?" Ricky asked me one day as we sat in their cluttered backyard. I could feel my face burning as his brothers awaited my response. I offered meekly, "Like, you mean, a cat?" causing them to burst out in laughter, kicking their legs in the air with glee.

It was Matthew, the middle one, who found a box of matches in the garage and said we should walk around looking for bugs to burn, a quest that got us as far as the bushes surrounding the elementary school when a police car came speeding up. Someone who lived across the street thought we were trying to set the school on fire and called the cops, who took down our names and called our parents to pick us up. My mom arrived first and glared at the Vickers, as if to emphasize that they were inherently to blame for all neighborhood disturbances, before turning her anger on me. I was in tears by that point, which she interpreted as genuine remorse. None of the other culprits had shed a tear. My dad showed up at our house a few hours later, but he didn't come in. He made me walk to the end of the driveway while he sat in his car. He was battling a receding hairline, but his new glasses and tailored suit offered sharp contrasts to our state of affairs on Lakepointe.

"What the hell is going on with you?" he asked me. "Isn't playing with matches pretty much the first thing kids are told not to do?" It seemed like a rhetorical question, so I didn't say anything. I just stood there outside his car door, like I used to do when I was welcomed inside.

"Answer me!" he yelled, which made me jump. Tears started to sting my eyes and I did my best to hold them back, not wanting to give him the satisfaction.

"I wasn't the one with the matches," I said. "I was just there, but I shouldn't have been."

"You're damn right you shouldn't have been. Do you have

any idea what it's like for us to get a phone call like that – to hear that our son is being held by police? Do you know how fast this is going to leak out and people are going to think there's something wrong with our family? Do you ever think about things like that?"

"There *is* something wrong with our family!" I shouted, and the tears started coming, for the second time that day. It scared me how powerless I was to stop them.

———————

By the time I entered high school, I had left hockey behind, a decision my father accepted as a consequence of shifting circumstance. My rebellious streak morphed into a realization that I could combine a love for sports with writing skills sharpened since grade school, when teachers would make me stand in front of the class, voice quavering, and read my stories. As sports editor of my high school newspaper, I penned an article about the football team, predicting Grosse Pointe South would fail to make the playoffs for the first time in four years. "Any resemblance this team has to the hard-charging juggernauts of years past is purely coincidental," I wrote, which angered the players, in particular linebacker Johnny Starrett, who characterized my analysis as "fucking horseshit" during a civics class we shared. "Kindly save your mindless machismo until the end of this period, Mr. Starrett," scolded the teacher, drawing guffaws from the rest of the class. When the Blue Devils won their season opener and carried their celebration into the locker room, a reporter from the Detroit News noted that they "tore a season preview from their own school's newspaper to shreds," oblivious to the fact that they would suffer a three-game losing skid at the end of the season to narrowly miss the playoffs.

By my second semester at Michigan State, I was working for the campus daily and taking it more seriously than most of my classes. The sports staff included Jesse Shears, a Black graduate of Detroit Southwestern whose glasses and beard made him look about 30 years old, which it turned out he might have been. The extent to which Shears strung out his college experience, taking just enough credits to still be classified as a student without graduating, was a well-worn newsroom narrative, I would soon learn. But first he had to welcome me to the fold. "I know you're from Grosse Pointe, so I'm not going to take anything for granted," he told me on my first day, to the delight of the other staffers. "I am a Black person. Do not be frightened. My name's Jesse and that over there is Tonya. I come from Detroit and she's from Saginaw. You might even meet some Jewish lads from suburban Chicago in your dorm or – watch out now – a Muslim honor student from Dearborn, like Khalil over here. You're not in Kansas anymore." We hit it off after that, with Jesse introducing me to coaches and athletes and tolerating my presence at parties where he worked as a DJ to make money on the side, playing his "house music" as students grinded into the night, another rationale for his extended campus stay.

When Michigan State made the Rose Bowl, we traveled to Pasadena along with Trevor Fitzgerald, a staff photographer who had a dependable car and the patience to deal with Jesse's demand to control the radio for the duration of the trip. The Collegiate didn't publish during Christmas break, so we had press credentials but no deadlines, which meant we partied the whole time. The night before the game, we drank beer and tequila at the hotel before making our way to the hot tub, joined by a group of girls who giggled as Jesse wailed obscene song lyrics. We had just started to broach the idea of taking the party to our room when a commanding voice said, "Out of the hot tub, girls...now!" It came from a man in a windbreaker behind us, arms angrily crossed.

"Excuse me," said the normally mild-mannered Trevor, slurring his speech. "What the hell is going on where you can just boss these ladies around?"

It was obvious the guy didn't feel the question deserved a response, but he offered one anyway. "Well, let's see, it's 2 a.m. and these ladies, as you call them, are high school students who are marching in the parade in about four hours, you absolute dipshit."

Once we returned to our rooms and Trevor passed out on the floor, Jesse and I lay in our beds, laughing about our failed womanizing during the trip and discussing tailgate plans for the next day. After a few minutes he turned serious, a rare enough occurrence to get my attention.

"How'd you get to be such a good writer, man? I wish I could write like you," he said.

I told him it came from reading, from my mother, who read to us every night when we were little, only turning the pages when she was sure we didn't have questions about the story. She didn't treat it as background noise, trying to get us to fall asleep. It was a shared experience.

"What about your old man?" Jesse said. "Was he a book nut, too?"

"Not really. He would read spy thrillers on his own,

but he was always busy with something else, chasing a new fad. He got into distance running and did a few marathons, then lost interest. Bought a sailboat and kept it down at the docks, taking us out every so often. Then he was going to be a beekeeper and had a few hives out in the middle of nowhere, where he tried to get me and my brother to put on suits to help him extract the honey. We wanted no part of it."

"If you knew some of my dad's hobbies," said Jesse, "you wouldn't be complaining."

"Well, the boat was definitely cool," I said, "but it seemed like he was working on it most of the time rather than sailing it. I do remember one trip we took on Lake Erie with some other families. We were on some remote island and all the kids were running around on rocks and I stumbled and fell on my head and cut it open. It was one of those jagged rocks. There was a flap of skin hanging on my forehead, basically. I never actually saw it."

"Wait a minute," said Jesse, sitting up in his bed. "You were on some island in the middle of nowhere and your head was split open? When the hell was this?"

"I think I was 7 years old. My mom was worried I would have brain damage, and she stayed down below with me as my dad and one of the other fathers sailed us to the nearest port that had a hospital. The reason I thought of this is that she was reading to me on the boat, just like I told you, and I corrected one of the things she said – she missed a word or something – and that's when she knew I was going to be all right, with no brain damage, as far as I know."

"Yeah, you turned out all right," said Jesse. "You'll be working at the New York Times and I'll still be playing my house music in East Lansing. That's how the shit's going to work. You're going to find your success, whatever that means."

He was starting to sound drowsy and soon he was snoring, but the words stayed with me. What did success mean for me? What had it meant for my father? Even after I moved to Sioux Falls and had a son of my own, the notion that my child's athletic achievements could be tied to my own happiness was not inconceivable, based on early experience.

Little League baseball was a natural starting point. Nathan and I spent countless hours playing catch, the pop-ups growing higher and more daunting until he could reach up with a glove larger than his head and snag the ball with regularity. I taught him to assess where the ball would land and get his body under it, rather than become hypnotized by its flight. His own throws were accurate enough that I rarely had to change my position. Then one day I was hitting grounders and a bad hop sent the hardball skidding into his shin, leaving him in the dirt howling loudly enough that bystanders came to check on his condition. "He'll be fine – just a weird hop," I assured them, but Nathan never looked at baseball the same way again. He was frightened of the ball, basically the death knell for a young player.

I signed him up for tackle football when he reached third grade, hoping for better luck. He played quarterback but was paired with kids a year older and more physically mature, and his coach admitted to being a novice at leading a team. No one learned how to block, and Nathan absorbed hit after hit, rising more slowly each time and inventing injuries to stay on the sideline. We switched to flag football after that and he played receiver, showing some of the hand-eye coordination that sparked his early baseball success. The Daily

Gazette had done a series on the danger of sports concussions, so I tried to put him off when asked about playing tackle football in high school. But when I heard that Brad Hawkins had requested his presence at offseason workouts and he was viewed as a potential contributor at receiver for a team with title hopes, we were excited about the possibilities. And now here he was, charging through ankle-high grass at the church lot, reaching up to snag another pass in front of his teammates and Cap Hawkins, who clapped me on the back before walking back to his truck. "Looks like we have ourselves a wideout," he said, and I allowed myself to acknowledge it was exactly what I wanted to hear.

FIVE

The mayor's office, on the first floor of an antiquated City Hall in downtown Sioux Falls, had been updated since my last visit. Plush carpet and padded chairs gave it a lavish appearance set off from the rest of the building, which was built before World War II and remained a relic of that age. In the corner of the office was a cherrywood desk polished with enough vigor to reflect the face of its 48-year-old occupant, Michael Harper, a political novice before he declared his self-funded candidacy for mayor in 2018 and silenced pundits by sweeping to victory. "Place looks a little different, right?" Harper said as I walked in. He had requested an off-the-record discussion, six feet apart with masks, and wanted to do it where he could show off renovations that took a year to complete. He wore a jacket but no tie and designer jeans, a stab at youthful finesse to balance the incursion of gray in his hair. His mask was adorned with the unofficial Sioux Falls flag. "Let me know if the sunlight bothers you," he told me. "I had these motorized blinds installed that are pretty handy. You need a water or something?" I declined and

then watched as he manipulated the remote control for the
blinds, cursing a few times before they climbed and plunged
at his command, which pleased him.

His expectation that things go according to plan dated
back to his previous job, as advance man for one of the banks
that established credit card operations in South Dakota but
headquartered in New York and elsewhere. Harper's role
was to lay the groundwork for the next location, traveling
around the country to sweet-talk local officials and ensure
that no messy regulations got in the way. It was an important
job that paid him well, he told reporters during his mayoral
campaign, but he couldn't escape the feeling that he was
destined for public service. He grew up in Aberdeen, South
Dakota's third-largest city, where he captained the debate
team in high school and faced off against his future wife in
competition. They wrangled over whether alcoholism was
a disease or moral failing, a subject of particular interest
to Harper since his stepfather was a problem drinker who
seemed unable to control his urges. "She was the best debater
on her team, and I won her over that day," Harper told the
Gazette for a profile. "I argued that scientific research showed
that changes in brain circuits caused a mental obsession with
drinking for addicts, rather than moral weakness or lack of
willpower. I talked about my stepdad and I could tell she felt
sympathy for my arguments – a no-no in debate but a good
quality in a person. We ended up going to my prom."

Harper's distaste for alcohol helped him buckle down at
the University of Minnesota, where he majored in business
but threw himself into student government, winning an election for president his junior year after spending three straight
days at the union with a handmade sign and a promise to give

students more of a voice. Bill Clinton had recently entered the White House, promising a "new covenant" filled with opportunity after the military entanglements of the Reagan/ Bush era. Tom Daschle, a graduate of the same high school as Harper, was increasing his influence in the Senate and would soon become majority leader. "I remember meeting Daschle at an event in Aberdeen," Harper told the Gazette, "and he didn't seem like a Democrat based on what I had been told Democrats were supposed to be. He wasn't talking about how government should tear up the system or take over our lives, but he did want to give everyone a shot at the American Dream if they played by the rules. It was corny but it worked for me. I thought we had a lot in common."

For one of his political courses in college, Harper drew up a campaign playbook around the premise that he would someday run for governor of South Dakota. The sections on fundraising, staffing and outreach ran more than a hundred pages, color-coded and annotated in a three-ring binder. But marriage and a baby girl came soon after earning his MBA, making earning a living more important than chasing a dream. As he settled his family in Sioux Falls and flew around the country, clearing obstacles for a billion-dollar subprime lending operation, the binder sat in the closet of his home office, a plan ready to be activated. "By the time I was 45 I decided I needed something else," he recalled. "I was tired from the road and wanted to spend more time with Cassie, our daughter. The thought of running for governor crossed my mind, but that seemed a daunting place to start. So I focused on mayor." He was among nine early candidates – city councilors, community activists, a former mayor, a teacher – and failed to get much traction until he started talking about getting a new events center built.

It had been a consistent failing of previous mayors to form a public consensus and figure out funding to replace the city's crumbling arena, forcing Sioux Falls residents to watch helplessly as conventions, concerts and sporting events leaked to surrounding states. I had written extensively about building a new multi-purpose facility at the existing arena site and connecting it to the convention center, rather than trying to shoehorn it into a downtown location. Polls showed that most citizens preferred to keep the project out of downtown because of the heavier price tag and parking and traffic woes, and Harper saw his chance. He jumped all over the arena site concept and promised to get the job done for just over $100 million and in his first term, angering downtown business owners who grumbled about their country club compatriot going populist. He held public forums to lay out his plan, sent out elaborate mailers and plastered billboards throughout the city with slogans (Hold Out for Harper!) that seemed hackneyed to his rivals but resonated with voters, as evidenced by a rise in the polls.

He finished second in the general election to set up a runoff with city councilor Kendall Merkens, a former college professor whose austerity on public spending earned him the nickname "Dr. No" and endeared him to older citizens who felt Sioux Falls was moving too fast. It was the perfect matchup for Harper, who knew that young professionals and even his ticked-off country club chums weren't going to align against optimism in the city's future, noting Merkens' insistence that sales tax revenue could dwindle in tough times. I thought about what a political consultant had told me about how Harper's candidacy gained steam. "He was showing up at all these parades, running around and shaking hands and handing out candy to the kids, and people were thinking, 'He doesn't have to be doing this. He quit a better job than the one that he's seeking. What's the catch?' Then it would dawn on them: 'He really wants this thing. My God, this is all real.'" By election night, when Harper soared to victory with nearly 60 percent of the vote and celebrated with his wife and daughter at a festive campaign headquarters, people were so taken by his enthusiasm in a largely non-partisan election that many didn't realize that they had just elected the city's first Democratic mayor in three decades. When he saw me at the victory party, gathering notes for a column, Harper put his arm around my shoulder and said, "We did it, man. We said we would get that damn events center built and now we're going to do it. How does it feel?" I could see a few of the TV reporters staring over at us, which led to an awkward exchange with Cummings in the newsroom the next day.

"Sounds like you're pretty chummy with our new mayor," he said, cornering me near the stairwell. "Is that going to be a problem?"

"Not sure I have time for this, Joe," I shot back. "Busy day today."

He tuned me out and kept talking. "I've heard some rumblings that he and his wife have holdings in a strip mall development and might be looking for some tax benefits on that. It's something we should keep an eye on."

He was wearing a sweatsuit that he donned about once a week, as if the Gazette's heavy lifting was part of his weight training. It increased my irritation. "So Harper hasn't even taken office yet and already he's committing ethical improprieties?" I said. "That's got to be some sort of fucking record.

How about we give the guy a chance to pick out the drapes in his office first?"

Cummings shrugged and walked off, and his tip about the strip mall fell flat. Harper made progress on his events center campaign promise, persuading the city council to sign off on consulting and design expenditures after heated public debate. When the pandemic reached South Dakota a year later, however, it created problems that even Harper's boundless enthusiasm couldn't conquer, putting most of his agenda on hold. He declared a state of emergency and briefly considered a citywide lockdown, but conversations with Governor Lawton's office steered him away from major restrictions. He wanted to pick his battles. Now, however, there was an outbreak at the Empire Foods pork processing plant across from the stockyards, one of the last vestiges of the city's meatpacking era. With nearly 4,000 employees, many of them immigrants or refugees, the virus was having a field day. The nature of the work made social distancing nearly impossible, and cases spiked to the point where the processing plant was the No. 1 hot spot in America, drawing the attention of the CDC and national media. It didn't surprise me, then, that the initial ebullience Harper showed while showing me his office waned by the time he sat down with a stack of papers on a couch near the windows, allowing circumstances to weigh him down.

"This thing has gotten out of hand," he told me. "I've got CNN and MSNBC asking for interviews so they can paint Sioux Falls as the Covid capital of the world, and Empire executives are slow-walking this thing. They're doing temperature checks at the employee entrance and handing out literature, but the shit is in English. You know how many languages are spoken inside that place? More than 80! They've got workers from Ethiopia, Nepal and El Salvador in there slicing up hogs, breathing on each other and then going home to cramped apartments, and they're handing out leaflets telling people to wash their goddamned hands!"

"Sounds like the cases are up over 600 today," I said. "What's the next move?"

"I'm sending a letter to Empire strongly suggesting that they shut the place down, just long enough to get the CDC in there so they can do a workplace analysis. I've talked to the union reps and think this is the best approach for now. We've already had one confirmed death of an employee from coronavirus. I reached out to the governor's office, because having her signature on that letter would carry a lot of weight, and that conversation just about ruined my day."

I asked him if he had spoken to Norah Newcombe, but I already knew the answer. "What the hell is her problem?" he said, raising his arms as if consulting a higher power. "She kept talking about how these were essential workers according to the Trump administration and that we needed to protect the vital food supply, and I'm thinking to myself, 'We might not have many people to feed if this outbreak spreads into the greater community,' which it almost certainly will. I really don't think Lawton and her folks view these workers as human beings. I had to keep reminding them that these are residents of the city of Sioux Falls. The union guy was telling me about one of the workers who tested positive – he's 50 years old from West Africa and worried about not getting paid if he stays away too long in quarantine. He's got five kids and his biggest fear is that his children will have to work in that place when they grow up. Do we force him to go back into a work environment that's not safe because he's not going to receive any support otherwise? Or do we shut things down, let the CDC get in there and urge the company to do the right thing for their employees in the meantime?"

His message must have resonated more than he thought, because a press release went out that afternoon from Lawton's office outlining a letter to Empire Foods signed by the governor and Harper, asking for a temporary shutdown of the plant to allow for federal inspections. We published an editorial the next day calling for greater action from state and city leaders, not just at the plant but with the overall Covid-19 response, which was too staggered and indecisive in the face of mounting urgency. Gina and I wanted to call for a statewide mask mandate, pointing to the rising percentage of positive tests, but Cummings talked us into softer wording that Lawton "strongly consider" action after reviewing data from other states. We also settled for language urging the governor to "move toward" restrictions for bars and restaurants, gyms, hair salons and recreational facilities. "You guys need to get off Twitter," Cummings told us on the Zoom call. "Basically no one I've talked to in the real world thinks it's a good idea to force people to wear masks. Lawton is trying to represent her constituents, which means listening to what they have to say." Gina, in a rare burst of frustration, pointed out that the governor's most fundamental responsibility was to protect her constituents, not coddle them, especially during a public health emergency. I could sense her waiting for me to override Cummings' assertions, particularly since we had him outnumbered, but I knew we would tackle this issue again and didn't want Cummings sulking about being silenced. I wrote a final draft that struck a balance between our arguments. "The most critical role of a governor in perilous times is to protect citizens from harm," the editorial concluded. "Even those who worship at the altar of 'personal liberties' want to see firm leadership when times get tough. They want messages of hope, but also admonitions of responsibility and sacrifice. They want to hear what the plan is."

About 20 minutes after the editorial posted online, I got a call from Norah Newcombe. "Did you meet with Harper yesterday in his office?" she asked me, skipping formalities. When I asked her where she had heard that, she said, "I'll take that as a yes. So much for Covid restrictions when it comes to sucking up to the mayor, I guess."

"I'm sorry," I shot back. "Is there a point to this phone call, other than you trying to piss me off?"

"As a matter of fact, there is. The point is that Mayor Harper wants to be the governor of South Dakota some day and is trying to do everything he can to make Governor Lawton appear incapable, including influencing editorials from the Gazette that are basically attack ads disguised as commentary."

"Is this some sort of joke?" I said. "You need to stop making wild accusations and start paying attention to the growing list of problems that South Dakota is facing. Turn on the national news to see how bad it is. And in the future, if you're tempted to spew this sort of bullshit in my direction, do yourself a favor and think twice before picking up the phone."

I went outside for some air, trying to make sense of what

I had heard. The extent to which Lawton had signed on to a peculiar political experiment was unsettling, and I wondered for a moment if she knew what she was in for. I recalled meeting with her when she was in Congress and disagreeing with her on many issues, but I never had the sense she would veer into commando politics, jockeying for far-right acceptance to fuel her ambition and ego. It all seemed perfectly Trumpian, which made sense because she served as a surrogate for his re-election campaign and was slated to speak at the national convention in August. But something about this was all her own, apart from Trump. Even after the president appeared in public several times wearing a mask, Lawton remained stubborn, insisting that people shouldn't be "shamed" into wearing face coverings in public, a stance cheered by conservative media. She traveled to GOP events in early primary states Iowa and New Hampshire, fueling speculation that she would run for president in 2024. This was a carefully crafted strategy that could not have only come from Newcombe. The prospect of national coordination, and a desire to make sure hard work didn't go to waste, partly explained why Lawton viewed Harper as a threat, because losing her re-election bid for governor in 2022 would be a shattering blow.

Disagreements about the government's role in dealing with the pandemic went beyond just the governor, though. Friction was everywhere, picking up where Trump's impeachment trial left off in February. Some national tragedies – Pearl Harbor, 9/11 – pull the country together in the face of a common enemy, until fresh divisions emerge. That grace period didn't exist with the coronavirus, nor was there any nuance. The virus was either a threat to the future of mankind or nothing worse than the flu. Shutting down businesses or events was either a prudent and science-driven gesture toward public safety or a drastic overreaction from health officials designed to control people's lives. Those who wore a mask and complied with restrictions were either responsible citizens or frightened sheep, fooled again by liberal politicians and media. Much of this discourse raged despite rising mortality rates, with South Dakota reaching its 100th coronavirus-related death in July and facing dire projections for the fall. It was natural, perhaps, to look at the pandemic through the lens of one's own existence, expressing frustration at the interruption of normalcy and questioning the need for extreme measures when the virus lurked outside personal parameters, a battle for strangers to wage. Increasingly, though, South Dakotans reached the point where they knew someone who "had it" and passed it to an acquaintance, and another, and another, until the ripples were so wide that apathy was no longer an option.

―――――

On our newsroom call with reporters the next day, Gina asked for fresh angles on the coronavirus, trying to find a feature for the "Covid Chronicles" series that had become popular with readers.

"There's a nursing home up in Watertown that's getting hit pretty hard," offered Patrick Schmidt, a business reporter who was focusing on pandemic coverage. "Not just because of at-risk residents, which is a big part of it, but also overworked staff, limited access to protective equipment and not a lot of cooperation from the state health department."

"Isn't that more of a straight news story?" asked Cummings.

"Yes, but also human interest," said Patrick. "To contain spread within these long-term care facilities, residents are asked to stay in their rooms at all hours, and family visits are put on hold, which means basically no human contact other than staff."

"Sounds depressing," someone on the call said. "Or more depressing, I guess."

I ignored that comment and kept things moving. "All right, so what's the feature angle here? Is there a family that's willing to talk?"

"Not only willing to talk, but with a powerful story," said Patrick, who had received a call from a woman whose 86-year-old grandmother was in the Watertown facility suffering from dementia. The caller's grandfather visited his wife every day before the pandemic, showing her family photos and telling stories to awaken memories of the moments they shared. When Covid restrictions began, the husband was forced to sit on a stool outside his wife's window, pressing photos to the glass and singing songs loud enough for her to hear. Some days her face appeared only sporadically, peering past him. On others she would strain from her chair and inch closer to the glass as he conjured images of their wedding, when her dress became tangled at the altar and as she became flustered, he whispered to her, "Pay it no mind. This is perfect." It was a story she likely would have shared at their 65th wedding anniversary if things had turned out differently, her granddaughter told Patrick. "The saddest thing I've ever seen was when he sang 'You Are My Sunshine' outside her window after she tested positive for the virus," he quoted her as saying in our front-page story that Sunday. "It was a dull overcast morning, I remember, and cars were going past, and I was thinking, 'This is too ordinary. Where are the rays of light? Why aren't the birds chirping?' Tears were streaming down his cheeks as he struggled through the song, realizing he would never embrace his wife again in this life, and the reaction from the world around him was like, 'Well, what did you expect? This is our reality now. We're all in this together, right?' She passed away two days later."

SIX

After practicing for 10 days in the August heat, the Edison Nighthawks were ready for action, suiting up for a scrimmage ahead of the season opener the following week, when classes started. Governor Lawton had been adamant that school should be in person and most districts had complied, often in the face of protests from unionized teachers and uneasy parents. In the spirit of the governor's laissez-faire doctrine, not to mention the threat of lawsuits, masks for students in Sioux Falls were not mandated but rather "expected." Screening for symptoms was coordinated with the state health department, with positive cases and close contacts quarantined and linked to remote learning. But skepticism remained high. As South Dakota barreled ahead with fall high school sports, ignoring the trend toward pushing activities into 2021 or cancelling them altogether, one football coach told me that the chances of getting through the season to the championships in November were "about the same as Lawton voting for Biden." Nearly six months into the pandemic, political humor was in vogue.

Edison's field was chalked up like a real game, with refs in uniform and the scoreboard reading 7-0 by the time I arrived from work. It was an exhibition against crosstown Westgate, with no spectators other than parents, but I cursed myself for being late. I spotted Nathan in his scarlet and gray No. 80 jersey standing on the sideline, fiddling with his mouthguard and chatting with teammates. He was shorter than a lot of the players but didn't seem out of place, which I had worried about. "I'm a possession receiver, Dad," he had informed me, invoking names like Wes Welker and Julian Edelman. "We're allowed to be short." By the time I climbed the bleachers to where my wife was sitting, she was talking to one of the other moms, ignoring the action on the field, a typical Connie move. She saw me coming and pointed theatrically to where her wristwatch would be, mainly out of habit. "Well, you missed Nate's first catch," she said, her sunglasses and mask making it hard to tell if she was actually annoyed. "It was a short one, not like a touchdown or anything. How many yards was it, Cara? Two? Three? No, it wasn't that many!" I let them sort it out as I took my seat, looking down to where Cap Hawkins was stationed in the front row with a companion who didn't look much like a football dad. The back of his T-shirt had a Harley-Davidson logo partly obscured by a ponytail, and he was poking at the air while speaking to Cap, who nodded before rising to his feet. Brad Hawkins had broken loose on a long run, tucking the football under his arm and decking a few defenders before finally being shoved out of bounds. The senior quarterback stood up quickly and taunted the Westgate players while tossing the ball at the referee and running back to the huddle, drawing a supportive whistle from his father, who brought his fingers to his mouth for extra volume.

"Looks like we have a good team," said Connie. "And some energetic parents," I replied. She reached over and took my hand, gripping it tightly. It was a humid day, but her shoulder-length blonde hair showed no signs of wilting, much to the dismay of friends who teased that her Nordic tresses were too perfect to be believed. I had the same reaction the first time I saw her at the Lantern, about five years after I moved to Sioux Falls. She was standing across the bar, laughing at someone's joke, and I pointed her out to Barry, a veteran Gazette copy editor and drinking companion. "Ah, the classic Norwegian beauty," he said. "A descendant of those hardened souls who weathered the wind-swept prairie to forge a new life. Quite a specimen, really. Blonde hair, finely proportioned facial features, amazing tits." I feigned outrage, saying, "Those are not tits, Barry. Those are breasts. Show them the proper respect." She approached me later that night near the jukebox, melting my earlier bravado into puddles of insecurity. I had not expected to speak with her.

"My friend says you've been staring at me all night," she said, swaying to the music in her sun dress, relishing my discomfort.

"I stare at a lot of things," I managed to say. "Some more sightly than others."

She laughed, sipped her drink, then flipped the script, staring at me for what seemed like a full minute without words, the buzz of the bar and Bob Seger's "Night Moves" as backbeat. "You're better-looking than your picture in the paper," she finally said, releasing the trance. Her eyes stayed on me, stirring adolescent anxiety as I leaned over to kiss her on the cheek.

One of our first dates was an overnight stay in Minneapolis, where I covered a basketball game involving a former South Dakota player and asked her to come along. After my assignment we hit the bars, easing inhibitions before careening into our hotel room and falling into each other on the bed. Her hair tickled my face as she leaned over me, our rhythms gaining urgency and volume before our bodies settled as one. "You've taken my virginity," I said to break the silence, and she giggled before rolling over to sleep. We both determined, I later learned, that the trip home would dictate our next move. If the connection was purely physical and our nearly four-hour ride was nothing but small talk and awkward silence, we would part ways and trudge on with separate lives. But the conversation flowed naturally, despite our hangovers, boding well for the future. She told me about growing up in Sioux Falls with basically a single mother, since her father, Raymond, suffered from paranoid schizophrenia and shuttled in and out of the veterans hospital, depending on whether he took his medication.

Raymond was divorced from Connie's mother and lived alone, so Connie's relationship to him was more care-taker than daughter, making sure he got his meals and took his pills and stayed out of trouble. Her mother worked for years as a receptionist at one of the local TV stations, spending many of her nights on hastily arranged dates with news anchors or their pals. Connie became an equal opportunity partier in high school, at home with jocks and potheads, and made headlines as a senior when she and her friend somehow got their car stuck on the railroad tracks near the stockyards and had to abandon it as a freight train, blaring its horn in vain, destroyed the Chevy Citation belonging to Connie's mom. "The headline in the Gazette the next day was, 'Teens nearly meet deadly fate on tracks,'" Connie told me. "I always thought it should have been, 'Teens avoid boo-boo from choo-choo.'"

She wished she had studied harder and not dropped out of college, because now she was stuck living with her mother and working at a credit card call center, taking questions from customers about late fees and minimum payments and annual percentage rates, thinking of anywhere else. "I'm going back to school to finish my degree," she told me. "I want to study more about literature. I love the idea of reading novels and then sitting in a big lecture hall where the professor lays out theories on what the author was trying to say and then we sort of give our opinions, and the conversation goes back and forth, with no right answers." By the time I dropped her off at her mom's house, I had told her about some of the discussions from my American Lit classes at Michigan State, from Hawthorne to Fitzgerald to Roth, and how much of that reading shaped my writing. I related how I had ended up in Sioux Falls, where my career aspirations weren't limited to sports reporting. And I explained how none of my family lived anywhere close to South Dakota, so she wouldn't have to worry about meeting them, at least for

a while. "You won't be so lucky," she said as she grabbed
her stuff and kissed me goodbye.

———————

The following week I met her father, who had slicked-back
silver hair and a wiry body that rarely remained still, a condition aggravated by illness but also his chronic consumption
of black coffee. During his manic states, Raymond fashioned
himself as a private dealer of used Cadillacs, which he would
acquire at auction and sell when he could turn a profit.
Finding a place to park them, and talking him out of buying
more, were tasks that fell upon Connie's mother, who made
sure her ex-husband's bills were paid out of his government
checks. A month after meeting Connie, I purchased a fair-con-
dition yellow Eldorado from Raymond, putting $1,000 down
with a handshake agreement to pay him $200 a month until
it was mine, a convenient way to rebound from my Ford Pinto
going kaput. The Cadillac seemed three times larger than my
old car, to the point where I was worried about hitting parked
cars or veering into oncoming traffic, and it was later stolen
from outside the Lantern when I left the ignition running on
a frigid December night, worried it might not start up again.
Long before that, Connie and I were having dinner with her
mother when Raymond, taking advantage of the open-door
policy, stormed in with a wild look in his eyes. He brushed
past Connie when she tried to cut him off in the kitchen and
started shouting at me, foam at the corners of his mouth.
"Where's my money, you son of a bitch! Who do you think
you're dealing with?" he yelled, until both Connie and her

mom were pushing him back toward the door.

He nearly struck a tree pulling out of the driveway and was back at the veterans hospital the next day, with a new round of antipsychotics. The Kentucky Derby was that weekend, and I knew that Raymond used to frequent racetracks in California when he served in the Navy, so I had an idea. I bought a $20 ticket for a horse that I thought had a decent shot to win the Derby and presented it to Raymond when Connie and I visited him that Saturday. We sat in the recreation room, where they had a workable TV, and watched the buildup to the race. Raymond was considerably more relaxed and mustered an apology for his actions as Connie reiterated our agreement on the Cadillac payments. He thanked me for the betting slip, holding it warily as the horses were placed in the starting gates, some of them putting up a fight. "They like to rear up when they see them gates," said Raymond, forcing a grin through his stubble. "Those jockeys need to yank on that halter or give 'em a taste of the whip." Connie bristled at that remark, but she was up and cheering when the race started and our horse bolted to an early lead, his purple and white colors untouched by the tumult behind. "Look at him go!" she cried, drawing a chuckle from her father. A few hospital staffers shuffled over to watch the action. Our horse still led the pack entering the final stretch, where he was pushed wide and started to fade, lost in the torrent as fresher legs pounded past, finishing seventh and ignored amid the fanfare for the Derby champion. Raymond, who had stayed calm throughout the race, rose from his seat, looked me in the eye and ripped the betting ticket in two before depositing in a trash can on the way back to his room. "Off to the glue factory," he muttered.

Connie and I moved into a small second-floor apartment in central Sioux Falls, endeavoring upon a level of domestication that our conflicting schedules and meager salaries allowed. Late-night carousing with friends on weekends was followed by mornings of sex and reading in bed, or movie marathons that contorted personal preferences into a collective, meaning it was no longer that "I" liked Woody Allen movies but that "we" liked some of them, forsaking early films that Connie dismissed as silly. She regarded employment as a nuisance that kept us apart, so when I dropped her off at the call center for morning shifts she would half-jokingly grab me with both arms and wail, "Don't make me go!" before snapping down the visor to check her makeup. On the rare instances when I didn't work nights at the Gazette, she would already be leaning out the apartment window by the time I exited the car, shouting "You're late!" and outlining plans for the evening, not willing to wait until I got inside. On one of those occasions, I handed her a takeout carton from a local restaurant and said, "I already ate – you want some?" which led to her grabbing the carton angrily out of my hands and tearing it open to find an engagement ring I purchased with my last remaining savings at the jewelry store in the mall. The diamond was blue topaz, a nod to her birthstone, and she dropped everything but the ring to the floor of our apartment, sobbing loudly enough that one of the other tenants came up to see if everything was all right.

We were married the following summer on Fourth of July weekend, which allowed my parents and Wayne to make the trip to

South Dakota, all on separate flights. My dad had relocated to Boston, near where he grew up, and was in between marriages. His third wife had been an antique dealer, and he continued to dabble in Victorian furniture and first-edition books until his next hobby or wife came along. Wayne had gotten his master's degree at Stanford and was working in northern California as a software engineer, too busy for romantic entanglements but the proud owner of two cocker spaniels. My mother remained in Grosse Pointe, married to a former middle school principal who made improvements to the Lakepointe house and owned a cabin up north for summer frolics. He was teaching my mom to play golf, a notable feat on its own.

At the rehearsal dinner, she pulled me aside to tell me how much she liked Connie, qualifying the praise somewhat by asking about her university credits. She then shifted to a soliloquy on the dangers of divorce until I cut her off by asking, "Mom, is that something to talk about the day before my wedding?" She had frosted her hair and cut it short, making the age around her eyes seem refined, and I hoped there were signs of happiness there. "I'm just saying that you must do everything you can to make it work," she told me. "Pay attention to her needs. Respect her opinions. Once you have kids, the damage that a broken marriage can do is real, and it never goes away." I realized that she was talking about me, the damage that I had incurred, and before I had a chance to ask for clarification, someone whisked me away for a toast to the bride and groom.

The pastor at Connie's Lutheran church refused to allow us to use the Beatles song "In My Life" in the ceremony because the lyrics include a reference to previous "friends and lovers," a concept deemed too scandalous. "Good thing you didn't choose 'Helter Skelter,'" joked Terry, who had driven up from Des Moines to be my best man. The day before the wedding, we had lunch and played volleyball in the pool behind Connie's aunt's house, with Terry and I dominating the competition. My dad stalked the deck in dress slacks and collared shirt, wisps of gray hair wavering in the sun. He couldn't help but analyze the action, especially when Wayne teamed up with one of Connie's friends and spiked the ball into the net on consecutive tries. "You've got to get higher out of the water, Wayne!" came the command. We tried to laugh it off, but Terry let Wayne have a few points just to take the heat off, sensing his irritation.

Connie was more concerned about her own father, who promised to take his meds so he could perform his paternal duties and walk her down the aisle. Terry and I saw him before the ceremony, looking fidgety but grounded in his tux, and he allowed me to straighten his corsage and wipe a trace of shaving cream from under his chin. He hadn't fulfilled the traditional role of a father, through little fault of his own, but the elemental instinct of wanting his daughter to be safe and happy still burned. "Do right by her," was all he said, and I assured him that I would. Later, as I stood at the altar and the organist thundered into the wedding march, I allowed myself to take my eyes off Connie for a moment to observe Raymond as he walked alongside his daughter, elbows locked, determined look on his face as he delivered her to the next stage of her life and then, unbeknownst to most everyone else, winked at me before retreating.

Freed from the bonds of censorship, we danced to "In My Life" at the reception, Connie in her wedding lace, bodies interwoven, thinking of love as something new. Her mom had suggested we take ballroom dancing lessons to choreograph our movements, but Connie shot the idea down. "We'll dance like we normally do," she said. "Holding on tight and making it up as we go." The sight of Wayne taking the floor for the second song, twirling Connie's former college roommate like he was Travolta, affirmed her faith in spontaneity. We partied well into the night and awoke early the next morning to a message that my dad was downstairs ready to check out and wanted to say goodbye. We walked dizzily down in our sweats and found him in the lobby, standing by his suitcase. I thanked him for coming, made a joke about the volleyball drama and reached to shake his hand, but he surprised me by pulling me into a hug, which led to Connie also being ensnared in an awkward group embrace, our heads bowed with something like reverence. After a few moments I realized my father was crying, his body racked by full-blown sobs, enough to draw stares from other early risers as he exclaimed how much he loved us and how much he'd miss us, and how we should cherish what we had. Connie shot me a look, uncertain how to react, and a few moments later my father was gone.

―――――――――

The gradual devolution of our marriage from nights of passion to stretches of celibacy was attributable to a variety of factors, including my work schedule and the fact that Connie was taking night classes to earn her college degree. Mainly, though, the fault was mine. I found myself coming up with reasons not to go to bed at night until she was asleep

– a book to finish or game nearing its conclusion. There was inherent pressure for men in sexual scenarios, I told myself, a need to perform, and our conjugal relations lacked a spark. I wondered how much my dad's transgressions and some of my own recklessness played a role in my view of sex as not a physical manifestation of love but a primal lurch into unforeseen consequences, much to Connie's alarm. She wanted to have children and she wanted a normal husband, not one who found excuses to avoid the marital bed. We tried to find diversions to spice things up, and sometimes they came unannounced. When I won the national award for our Gazette series on the governor's use of state aircraft, the honor included an expense-paid trip to Washington D.C. for the ceremony, with spouses included. The reception took place at the Hyatt Regency near Capitol Hill, where we mingled with other journalists during cocktail hour, wearing name tags to facilitate conversation. When Connie excused herself to go get another drink, I heard one of the women murmur to her companion, "Well, she definitely wins the hair award." I started chatting with a Chicago Tribune columnist whose name I recognized, and when Connie returned, she asked him if he had to work a lot of night shifts on the desk like I did. "He's a Pulitzer Prize winner," I snapped. "I don't think that's a big concern." The guy tried to lighten the mood by joking about the crazy hours that any journalist keeps, but he soon made his escape and Connie was cool to me for the rest of the night.

As soon as we returned to our hotel room, exhausted from the fanfare, she started in. "Can I ask you a question?" she said. "Do you really have to treat me like an idiot in front of other people? I mean, does it give you some form of pleasure?" I replied that it did not. "OK, then, what does give you pleasure? I'd really like to know." I told her that it would have pleased me if I could have cashed my $2,500 award check at the front desk of the hotel, as I attempted unsuccessfully, with the Chicago Tribune reporter looking on. That made her smile, grudgingly, providing the real answer for what gave me pleasure. We watched a movie before we dozed off, maintaining our recent ritual of separate beds. It was Connie who bridged the divide, pulling back her covers and crawling under mine, clad in just her panties, leaving nothing to chance, taking us back to that night in Minneapolis when we let down our defenses and explored each other's bountiful terrain. The release we experienced increased our exhaustion, and as we lay there, waiting for sleep, I heard her say, "We just made a baby," in barely more than a whisper.

When the scrimmage ended, we both headed down to the field to meet with Nathan, who had two catches in Edison's 35-7 victory and was eager to get into the locker room. "I'll be there in a minute!" he called to one of the linemen before accepting a hug from Connie. He had a few grass stains on his knees but was otherwise unmarked by his efforts.

"Not exactly an offensive masterpiece," I told him, "but not bad for the first time out."

"Just an exhibition, Dad," he replied. "Mainly to work through some stuff. I think Brad's going to be running a lot, especially on third down, so I don't know how many targets I'll get."

He gave a high-five to another teammate walking past while waiting for my reaction.

"What kind of attitude is that?" I said. "He's going to have to throw the ball sometime, and somebody's going to have to catch it when he does."

I saw Nate's eyes drift to someone behind me and felt a heavy hand come down on my shoulder, leaving little doubt as to the person's identity.

"Absolutely right!" said Cap Hawkins as he came into view, mask around his chin. "Brad needs to show off his arm for the colleges anyway, and I wouldn't want him to get too banged up. I told him, 'Boy, you can't just take off at the first sign of trouble. Stay in that pocket and trust your receivers!' You'll get your chance, son."

The last remark was for Nathan, but Cap was looking at Connie, waiting for an introduction. I was about to offer it when she spoke up. "I'm Connie, Nathan's mom. So what do you do, Cap? When you're not whistling really loud, that is."

"Well, you got me on that one!" he said with that gravelly laugh. "I get carried away at these dang games and can't help but make a racket. Brad keeps telling me to pipe down, but I am what I am, I guess. I've got a small engine repair shop not far from downtown, working on snowblowers and lawn mowers and whatnot. If you guys ever need anything, I'm there most of the time." He saw Brad and kept moving, thumping me on the shoulder one more time, and we said our goodbyes to Nate as he trotted toward the locker room with helmet in hand. "That was fun," said Connie, lowering her mask to give me a kiss as I made my own exit, grateful that the pace of the day and the late-summer heat showed merciful signs of receding.

SEVEN

The car approached slowly before making a wide loop and coming to rest, engine still running. It looked like a BMW or Audi or one of those brands that used to bother me as a Detroiter before "American made" became difficult to divine. "About time," I muttered from my perch in the picnic shelter at Chatham Park, a collection of softball fields on the city's west side, where Mayor Harper and I had been scheduled to meet at 7 p.m. It was now 7:23, and he was rummaging through papers in his vehicle, using the dome light to fend off the dusk. This was our second clandestine meeting at the park, which Harper chose because it was on his side of town and devoid of activity once summer ended. The picnic shelter bordered a parking lot at the end of a winding road, far from neighboring houses, the sort of refuge where disaffected teens gather to smoke pot, keeping their music low. It would not have been my first choice for a place to spend my Wednesday night, but Harper promised a scoop for the Gazette.

Our initial meeting occurred in February of 2019,

during the state legislative session, when Governor Lawton
was blocking a bill that would have permitted cities to
exceed state-imposed sales tax ceilings, allowing Sioux Falls
to pursue some of Harper's spendy proposals. The mayor
handed me a folder with printed emails from the governor's
office, letters from supportive legislators and details of a
planned interchange that could spur development if the law
passed. It was good information that we later used, making
sure to contact other parties involved, but it was nothing
explosive. When I told Harper that it might seem untoward
for the news director of the Gazette to hold secret meetings
in a city park with the mayor, he said he couldn't hand over
documents at my office or his, and email was out of the question. "Didn't you ever see 'All the President's Men'?" he said
at that first meeting. "Who was the reporter that Robert
Redford played...Woodward? OK, well, he met his Watergate
source, Deep Throat, in a parking garage in the dead of night,
right? Work with me here. If you think I'm going to email
this stuff and have it exposed by a FOIA request down the
line, you're crazy." I tried to explain that Deep Throat was
offering information about a pattern of crimes and cover-
ups that ultimately toppled the Nixon presidency, whereas
Harper was trying to change a state law to build an offramp,
but that was before the pandemic hit. Now every day seemed
like Watergate.

    September in South Dakota had been brutal, expanding
the schism between those who took the virus seriously and
others who insisted the crisis was overblown, following the
lead of their governor and President Trump. Positive cases
spiked with the flow of college and high school students back
onto campus and the hands-off approach Lawton used to

enhance her brand among MAGA faithful. She made head-lines by allowing a motorcycle rally to proceed on the western part of the state, a festival of Harleys and hedonism that packed more than 450,000 people into a town of 7,000 residents, with masks a limited accessory. Reporters trying to pin down the governor found that she spent much of her time on the road, stumping for Trump in battleground states as conditions worsened at home. Covid was not just a Sioux Falls problem anymore, or Minnehaha County. Cases were rising throughout the state, confounding armchair epidemiologists who predicted the virus would spare areas with low population density, providing a natural buffer for South Dakota. Hospitalizations and deaths spiked exponentially, stirring anxiety in the state's relatively populous southeast corridor. Sioux Falls, the state's economic engine, contained pockets of progressivism, as well as two major health systems and a Democratic mayor. Calls grew louder for an aggressive mitigation strategy to offset apathy in Pierre, while conservative diehards warned of rocking the boat, noting that Trump won Minnehaha County by 14 points over Hillary Clinton in 2016. When Harper finally exited his car and headed toward me, clutching a manilla folder, his customary bounce had given way to the anguished stride of a man in a pandemic-fueled political pinch.

"Sorry I'm late," he said. "I know you hate doing this."

"Maybe I should have brought a joint," I replied.

"Huh? Oh, sure, I guess that makes sense in a setting like this. Never my thing, thankfully."

He hoisted himself so he was sitting on one of the picnic tables, knees rocking slightly. He had shed his sport coat, and his tousled hair no longer seemed an attempt at style but rather a casualty of mounting concerns.

"We had a park like this near my house in Aberdeen where my friends and I would play for hours, just making up rules as we went along," he said. "The glory days, right? I was never a great athlete, so I sort of turned myself into the idea guy. 'Here's a new game we can play, here's how it works, here's what the teams are.' My buddies didn't mind because they didn't have to worry about keeping score or anything. They let me do my thing. Then a new kid moved into town from Colorado one summer – his name was Jamie Daniels – and he could run faster than anyone else, he could throw a curveball and he had ideas of his own. We were probably 10 years old, and I hated this kid with a passion. We got into arguments about the rules for baseball and how to pick teams and one day he just threw his glove down and challenged me to a fight. My friends and I weren't really brawlers, so I sort of said, 'What?' And he said, 'Let's fight.' And I wish I could say I took him up on it and beat the hell out of Jamie Daniels right there on the playground, but that didn't happen. I tried to talk my way out of it, put a spin on it, but I could hear kids whispering that I was chicken, even a few girls that had gathered around. Some of my friends snickered as I walked away and headed home, and things weren't quite the same when school started up that fall. Maybe that's why I ended up in debate."

His eyes scanned the surrounding trees instead of looking at me, but I felt compelled to respond. "So whatever became of Jamie Daniels?" I asked.

"Homecoming king. Star quarterback. I think he's an investment banker now."

"Let me guess the moral of the story," I said. "Always

beat up someone from Colorado when you have a chance."

He smiled and reached for the folder, sifting through its contents while thinking about how to proceed.

"The situation with the governor's office is getting bad," he finally said. "Every time I tried to follow up on the Empire Foods plant, pushing to make sure they made the safety improvements the CDC requested, I was told to back off. The state health department tried to do contact tracing and put some family members in hotels, but Norah Newcombe's talking point was, 'Just get the plant running again. We need to keep feeding people. This is what the White House wants.' I've included some of those messages in here. You can use them as a starting point. I also talked to some of the hospital administrators in town, who say they're fearful of speaking out in favor of statewide restrictions because it might jeopardize some of the federal Covid funds Lawton's office is doling out."

"Did the governor actually tell them that?"

"Not in so many words, but the pressure is there. They went along with that stupid hydroxychloroquine trial, which shows how much they feel like their hands are tied. Now I'm starting to look like a jackass because neither the governor's office nor the hospitals will listen to me."

"You want to start making the rules again," I said.

He allowed himself a weary smile. "Maybe there was a point to that story. Maybe I am ready to fight. In the business world, I had control over what course I wanted to take and could trust my instincts. At the very least, I'm planning to get the city council on board for a mask mandate in Sioux Falls to get things under control. The language is in this packet. I'm also looking at the schools, which is going to be a tough one. I'm talking to board members about possibly shutting down public high schools and middle schools and going back to remote learning in our district."

It took a few moments for his words to sink in, and my mind went to football. Edison had started the season 4-0 and Nathan was becoming more utilized in the offense, with three catches in his last game. The season had been a bit of an adventure – several schools forfeited games because too many players were positive cases or close contacts – but it hadn't been the outright disaster some predicted. If anything, there was a growing determination among coaches, athletes and parents to finish out the year as proof that not every facet of their lives was controlled by the virus – a rare victory amid a succession of losses.

"What about athletics?" I asked Harper. "A lot of the seasons are in full swing."

"You really can't continue with activities if you're not doing in-person classes," he said. "Fall sports would be interrupted, which mainly impacts – wait, your son is playing for Edison this year, right? I forgot about that. Good for him. Well, it's not a done deal yet, and there's a possibility they can pick things up in the spring. It's like you guys have been saying in your editorials, sometimes it's about sacrifice. My wife and I were planning to take our daughter and one of her friends on a trip to Mexico in December, and guess what? That's not happening. We learn to live with the hand that we're dealt."

"I agree we all have to sacrifice," I said. "But it's also important not to overreact."

"This is not overreacting," he said, a little abruptly. "This is an attempt to act, for Chrissake. It's fine for Lawton to do nothing in her own state while shilling for Trump all over the map, refusing to wear a mask, because she's got people thinking that's leadership, believe it or not. Welcome to the Grand Old Party! I don't have that luxury, and she and Newcombe are making me look like a chump, just daring me to do something unpopular. Well, real leaders aren't afraid to do the unpopular stuff, especially during a crisis." He rose from the table, energized by his rant, and handed over the folder before heading to his vehicle. "You didn't get that from me," he called over his shoulder.

As soon as I got home, I arranged a Zoom huddle with Gina and Patrick, who had done a nice job on the nursing home stories. Cummings was coming off consecutive night shifts and I decided not to bother him, partly for my benefit. I wasn't eager to explain to him where I got the documents and face more questions about my Harper connection, though I knew Gina would fill him in. The sad truth was that we weren't going to get these stories through official channels in South Dakota, where government restrictions were tolerated when it came to accessing public records. I opened the meeting by talking about the mask mandate proposal that would go before the city council the following week, calling for face coverings to be worn indoors in places open to the public where a six-foot distance could not be maintained.

"They'll have to take public input on this," said Patrick. "That should be interesting. I expect a lot of people not wearing masks complaining about masks in a place that does not yet require masks. Good times, for sure."

"Depending on how packed that building gets, you might want to just follow the livestream," I said. "Out of an abundance of caution, as they say. It should be a close vote, and Harper will have to break the tie if it ends up 4-4."

Gina questioned the level of suspense in that scenario, since Harper was the one making the proposal. "Wouldn't it be a slam dunk?" she asked.

"Not necessarily," I said. "I sort of sense he wanted to bring this to council to show that he's taking the matter seriously and wants to control the spread, but he still wants to read the room. If you get enough people threatening to burn the house down if it goes through, we'll see if he blinks. And if the mask mandate happens, shutting down schools could be next."

"Wait, what?" said Gina. I had forgotten she knew the education beat as well as anyone. "Where did you hear that?"

"I've got my sources," I said lamely. "Right now, it sounds like Harper and his team are just thinking about it, waiting for more data. It's something we need to keep an eye on, but it's not a story yet."

I could see Gina's face contort a bit as she considered that last statement. She had a habit of moving closer to the screen when she had an important point to make, which in volleyball they called going for the kill.

"Well, if we don't have a single source on the record, it's definitely not a story," she said. "The mayor typically doesn't control the school district, but everything changes during public health emergencies. He probably has the power to shut it down, as mayors have elsewhere, but it would be a radical move. We'll start sniffing around without giving the story away."

Before we signed off, I shared images of the emails pertaining to Empire Foods and the governor's reluctance to challenge the company. I told them that it was all background at this point, but the emails formed the nucleus of a story showing the difference between Lawton's public pronouncements about plant safety and her private eagerness to get the place up and running, regardless of CDC concerns.

"We could talk to the union reps and see if protocols are being followed," said Patrick. "Sounds like folks are fired up about how things went down. I covered a memorial a few months back for a guy who worked at the plant for 40 years, starting on the line and working his way up to shift manager before dying of Covid. He was 61 years old and getting close to retirement, but he came home feeling sick one night and died in the hospital a week later."

"Jesus," I said. "How did I not know about this? Did we cover the funeral?"

"They couldn't have one. His sister-in-law organized a drive-by visitation instead. People drove past and held up signs and honked their horns to pay their respects, just waves of cars. Motorcycles, too. He worked there four decades and had his retirement party and memorial all in one shot, and nobody could hug anybody. His wife just stood there and waved. The guy captained the plant's bowling team, and we ran a photo of his teammates walking past the house in their team shirts, carrying a sign that said 'R.I.P. HAMMER' – his bowling nickname."

Gina chimed in to make a point about the emails. "I'm going to take a wild guess that we got these from the mayor himself," she said. "Actually...wait...don't even answer that. I'm just wondering if we're going to open ourselves up to valid criticism if we use this stuff, like we're working one side. This is the news division we're talking about now, not edit board."

I saw Patrick avert his eyes from the coming storm as I pondered how to respond. The constant questioning of my news-gathering methods was getting old, especially since these were legitimate stories that were falling into my lap. Was the industry in such great shape that we could turn down exclusives about the state's most powerful people because we were squeamish about the appearance of subjectivity?

"Appreciate the journalism lesson, as always," I said to Gina. "Jesus, it's just like Cummings is here. We're not using the emails verbatim – our source won't allow that. We're using them as a starting point to tell the story of Lawton choosing the financial and political benefits of keeping the plant open over the safety and well-being of those who work there. If further reporting does not bear that out, then we won't run that story. Are we clear?"

I signed off abruptly, the equivalent of slamming the phone, and worked for another hour before heading upstairs. Nathan was at the kitchen table, doing homework but also checking his phone like a nervous tic, wary of missing out. There was a forum among football players that stayed active at all hours, mainly with inspirational nuggets – "Respect the Grind!" – from senior leaders. Lately the messages gained urgency, Nathan had told me that morning. Edison's next game was an intracity clash with undefeated Catholic Central, ranked right behind the No. 1 Nighthawks, and trash talk was running rampant. I watched Nathan shift from a worksheet to his phone, hair falling over his eyes, typing furiously before drifting back to his task.

"Maybe you should put the phone away when you're

doing homework," I said, grabbing a bottle of water out of the fridge. He didn't bother to look up.

"Just a little math," he said. "Almost done." We both knew his accelerated geometry had progressed past the point where I could help him, so I switched gears to find common ground.

"Any more back and forth with the Central kids?" I asked. This time he looked up and grinned, amused by my interest in social media chatter.

"It's getting pretty intense," he said. "Someone from Central posted something about Brad Hawkins getting busted for drinking last year. It was a photo of him holding a football, but they superimposed a whiskey bottle on there."

"How industrious of them," I said, pulling up a seat across from him.

"It was pretty funny, actually," said Nate. "Of course, Brad flew off the handle and started posting anti-Catholic stuff and threatened to beat everyone up after the game, or during the game, I guess."

None of that surprised me based on what I'd heard about Hawkins or seen from his father, but I didn't want to demean Nate's teammate more than the kid had managed himself. "I hope you're staying away from that stuff," I said.

Nate smirked while scribbling at his worksheet, multi-tasking again. "No one really cares what I think, Dad. I'm just some scrub receiver, remember? I'm just glad we're in school and not doing online classes."

I asked him about protocols and if kids were wearing masks. On the rare occasions when I dropped him off at school, I was pleasantly surprised by the amount of students who were masked up as they hauled their backpacks through the parking lot. I wondered how my generation would have responded to the same expectations.

"There are a few MAGA nuts who refuse to wear masks," said Nathan. "One kid in my English class walked out when the teacher showed a video about the Black Lives Matter protests over the summer, saying we were being brainwashed, and he's not alone. You'd be surprised how many Trump lovers there are at Edison."

"Does that include football players?" I asked.

"I'm sure it does, but they all want to keep the season going, so they go through the motions. Coach Talley keeps telling us if we follow the protocols, we've got a better chance to avoid being a close contact and we can stay on the field."

The school district had changed its policy on close contacts, lowering the threshold for quarantine if the student exposed was wearing a mask at the time. Positive cases were still required to stay home at least 10 days, and there were rumors that some athletes and even coaches hid their symptoms at the risk of exposing others.

"You guys have a good thing going," I said, grabbing some of his discarded wrappers to throw away. "It would definitely be a shame if someone pulled the plug at this point."

He looked up and met my gaze for the first time. "Who would pull the plug on it?"

I thought about bringing up my conversation with the mayor, but I couldn't risk Nathan telling one of his friends and having it leak all over social media. I threw the wrappers in the trash and gave him a reassuring smile on my way out of the kitchen.

"No one's going to pull the plug," I told him. "Forget I brought it up."

EIGHT

A few blocks from the heart of downtown, Sioux Falls shed the underpinnings of its past. The city acquired 10 acres of land from the rail company whose trains cleaved through the area for decades, carrying grain and livestock and later crude oil and ethanol. City planners turned around and sold those parcels to developers who shared their vision of upscale retail, paving the way for ale houses, sushi bars and boutiques that provided a trendy alternative to chain restaurants by the mall. If the railyard district didn't replace the warehouses, shelters and Salvation Army outposts from pre-banking boom days, it at least pushed them from the public square, where would-be bourgeoisie came to shop and play before retreating to their enclaves.

Cap Hawkins' repair shop existed on the fringes of this revival, near the viaduct that carried traffic over the rails. My lawn mower was acting up and he gave me a time to drop it off, insisting that early evenings worked best. I drove past facades for a bakery and apothecary before spotting a brown stucco building with boarded-up windows and a sign touting small engine repair and sand blasting. There were trucks parked in back, near a rusted shed and "no trespassing" signs, a curious way to make customers feel welcome. I unloaded my mower and wheeled it to a sliding door, which opened to the acrid odor of gasoline and rotten grass. Dozens of mowers and snowblowers were lined up with numbered tags, indicating either booming business or sluggish service.

"Well, well, well – there he is!" said Cap, standing behind a counter and wiping his hands with a rag. He was talking to both me and someone lingering near the back who turned out to be Dale Burgess, Tommy's dad. "This here's the famous journalist I've been telling you about," Cap told him. "His son's a pretty good receiver, too. We'll need all hands on deck to beat Central on Friday, am I right?" As I fidgeted with my mask and slid the mower into an open spot, I realized they were waiting for an answer. "It's No. 1 vs. No. 2," I said of the matchup. "Central has a pretty good defense, as usual, but I think we can move the ball on them."

"Damn right we can," said Dale, walking over to introduce himself. "If we can get the coach to mix up the plays and run the fucking ball, I think we'll win by two touchdowns." Cap started laughing, looking for my reaction while rubbing his oil-stained hands. "Imagine the dad of the running back wanting to run the ball more, right? What a shocker! Tommy will get his touches, but don't be surprised to see Brad chucking the ball around on those guys. I'd say the whole damn playbook is open."

He walked over to check the spark plug on my mower and asked a few questions before sticking a tag on it, promising to get to it quickly. He then waved us toward the back corner of the shop, stepping around mower blades and discarded tools to a door with an "Employees Only" sign. "This is where the magic happens," grinned Cap, opening it to reveal a room with a table and chairs and newspaper clippings tacked to the wall. There were two men at the table, one of whom I recognized as the guy with the ponytail sitting with Cap at the scrimmage. He was eating something from a plastic bag while arguing with the younger man next to him, turning without surprise when we entered the room.

"Cap, will you explain to the boy that this here is deer jerky, not beef," he said. I realized that the bearded younger man was probably his son. "He needs some enlightening."

"Ah, the serious questions of the day," said Cap, switching on another light. "That is indeed venison, shot by yours truly. We'll let the kid taste pheasant jerky pretty soon – the opener's not far off."

I was the only one wearing a mask and pointed out that I wanted to keep some distance, eliciting a groan from Dale. Cap shot him a look and spoke up. "If the man wants distance, we need to give him distance," he said. "He knows a lot about this stuff because of what he's been covering in the paper, assuming you guys can read." He introduced his ponytailed acquaintance as Ed and the son as Eddie. They each gave a slight wave.

"Ed's got South Dakota ties," said Cap, easing his large body into a chair with a groan. "Lives out in Michigan now, but we stay in touch through social media and other channels. That Governor Whitmer out there gives us a lot to talk about, shutting down businesses and keeping people locked in their homes to hide from the virus, all for her liberal bona fides. People are fed up. We started a group called F.A.R. – Freedom Against Restrictions – to deal with some of this stuff and air our views. Ed wanted to name it Freedom Against Restrictions Today, but I told him that would spell F.A.R.T."

They all laughed, and he leaned over to playfully punch Ed in the arm. "Sort of an inside joke for us," Cap said. "Anyway, these guys have been to a few rallies at the state capitol in Lansing, and they'll be at the city council meeting here in Sioux Falls. We're a little concerned about what our Democrat mayor is starting to cook up – seems a long way from what Governor Lawton intends for this state."

I had drifted to the corner to maintain some separation, probably pointless with the lack of ventilation in the room. Maybe gas fumes can kill off the virus, I thought. A glance at the wall revealed clippings from Detroit newspapers about Whitmer and one from the Gazette about Harper's mask proposal, with sections highlighted and circled. They were waiting for me to respond.

"I think the mayor feels that he's being forced to do something because our governor is missing in action when it comes to pandemic response," I said. "She keeps saying she's going to look at the science and data…well, the numbers show an increasing amount of people in South Dakota getting sick and going to the hospital. Some are dying."

"Old people are dying," said Ed, shifting in his chair to face me. He pushed the bag of jerky toward his son, who fished around for a piece. "Old people with conditions that would have likely caused them to die anyway. Are those Covid deaths or just deaths? Who can tell? The flu kills a lot of people, too, but you don't see us shutting down our country for it."

I had encountered the flu comparison many times from readers and batted it down with ease, but I held my tongue this time. Ed was just getting started. "Did you know that people are being put out of business in Michigan because of a power-hungry Democrat trying to play God?" he said. "It's estimated that a third of family-owned restaurants could run aground, not to mention hair salons and bowling alleys and movie theatres and fitness centers. A restaurant owner in my town was fined six thousand dollars for serving regular customers – people who had being eating there for more than 30 years. A barber in Owosso got shut down by state officials for giving haircuts to folks who chose to be in that chair. These are people who just want to make their own decisions about what is harmful to them and what is not. Freedom over tyranny – that's what it comes down to."

"Amen," said Eddie. "We oughta put it on a T-shirt." His father nodded thoughtfully, as if weighing merchandising options.

"A lot of those businesses are getting federal money to make ends meet until they can safely open again," I said. "I know times are tough, but…"

"They don't want handouts!" shouted Ed. "They want their lives back. They want dignity."

I thought back to the Michigan rallies and wondered if he was one of the protesters, some of them armed, who breached the state capitol in Lansing to confront legislators, a scary scene that drew national attention.

Before I could ask, Cap stood up and flashed the universal sign for timeout, trying to defuse the situation. "Hold on here now," he said. "I think we're all on the same team. Ed just wants to make sure that both sides are being presented because a lot of people are hurting. If the Gazette keeps running editorial after editorial blasting Lawton and calling for more action, Sioux Falls might end up like Michigan, with no freedom and no high school football. These 'Covid Chronicles' you guys keep running are pulling on my heartstrings, don't get me wrong, but we don't want Harper getting the idea that he's the next Gretchen Whitmer."

"I don't think that's what Harper wants to do," I replied. "I talk to him a lot. Sometimes we meet away from everything and shoot the breeze, and he's just frustrated, that's all." I saw Cap exchange a look with Ed when I mentioned the meetings – probably a mistake on my part. "He's getting it from both sides and wants to do the right thing."

"Well, I don't trust the son of a gun," said Dale, who had been quiet since we entered the room. "Worked for a credit card company all those years and now he's an expert on viruses and masks, going against our governor. Doesn't sound like he really understands South Dakotans."

Ed saw an opening to ask me where in Michigan I came from, and I told him Grosse Pointe. He sneered and told Dale, "That's where the upper crust lives, in case you didn't know. Looks like another guy who doesn't understand what South Dakotans really want."

That was about it for me. As I headed for the door, I noted my salary at the Gazette didn't qualify as "upper crust" and that I had been living in South Dakota for nearly 30 years, giving me plenty of insight into the hearts and minds of its citizens.

"Have you been on a pheasant hunt?" Cap asked me, and I admitted I had not. "Well, we might need to fix that. The opener is coming up, and hitting the fields is a great way to learn about hearts and minds – and maybe a few other parts of the anatomy." They all snickered at that as I made my out of the room, eager to find some fresh air.

The next time I saw them was at the city council meeting, where several hundred people showed up for public input on Harper's mask proposal at Thompson Hall, a former public library used as council chambers. Patrick had planned to cover the meeting remotely, but the livestream was so choppy that he ended up going in person, and I followed suit. "Welcome to paradise," he said when we met near the entrance. I looked past him to see the room completely full, with folding chairs used for spillover seating in the lobby. Many of the attendees were dressed in red while carrying signs (*Masks Are for Villains*) that they held up for the cameras. "Is anyone here to support the mandate?" I asked Patrick, who was masked up and looking a bit anxious. "The people who support it take social distancing seriously and want no part of this circus," he told me. "That makes it a home game for the anti-maskers." I saw Cap and Ed standing in the corner, wearing F.A.R. caps along with some of their companions. The merchandising had apparently begun. Other than media, city personnel and the councilors themselves, very few face coverings could be seen. "We've got ourselves a super-spreader event," I murmured to Patrick, who nodded warily and kept taking notes. Harper took his seat, with four councilors on each side, and gaveled in the meeting. He laid out the ground rules for public input, explaining that profanity, personal attacks and blatant misinformation were prohibited, adding that there were many false claims being circulated in the community. "Most of them are coming from you!" someone said, drawing shouts of assent as a police officer leaned over, looking for the culprit. Harper banged the gavel again and called for order, settling for a low murmur that pervaded the room. He was wearing his flag mask again, and as he scanned the crowd his eyes seemed to concede that college student government had not prepared him for what was about to unfold.

One by one, attendees walked to the podium and used their allotted five minutes to rail against the mayor's proposal. Some read from notes and others turned to incite the crowd, seeking affirmation or applause before being reminded to address the council. One man, wearing a red "Freedom First" shirt, declared that the coronavirus was a government-fueled hoax meant to control the populace and further enrich the pharmaceutical industry, claims quickly fact-checked by the mayor. Next up was a woman who downplayed the dangers of public gatherings without a mask, gesturing around the room for emphasis. "Everyone in here should have the freedom to assess our own level of risk as we go about our lives," she said. "How much are we willing to accept? Me personally, I believe I have a greater chance of getting struck by lightning than contracting the China virus." One of the councilors responded by pulling up data on lightning strikes compared with Covid numbers to refute her assertion, leading to a chorus of boos and more gavel pounding from Harper, whose patience was waning. Several councilors raised questions about how the mandate would be enforced, expressing concern about "folks calling the cops on each other" for not wearing a mask, saying it would heighten tensions. That was followed by the city's public health director, who pointed to increased community spread and said hospital officials were expressing concern about the availability of intensive care beds, to which several cries of "Fake news!" rocked the chambers. I noticed that Cap and Ed joined the chorus but remained in the corner of the room, not approaching the lectern.

"Thank God this shit show is almost over," Patrick leaned over to tell me. "I think it's time to vote." There was a brief discussion with the city attorney on the legality of the ordinance before councilors began rendering judgment, ignoring shouts from the gallery while producing an expected deadlock – four in favor and four opposed. All eyes were on the mayor, who had clasped his hands before him during the votes like a man in solemn prayer. He was not a religious man, he had told me, and any notion of divine intervention sparing him from casting the tiebreaking tally had vanished. He sorted through notes before leaning toward the microphone, addressing a room that even the most jarring of objectors had allowed to fall silent. "This is a tough vote for me, as you can probably imagine," he began. "It's been hard for me as mayor to see the pain this virus has inflicted upon our city at a time when we should be experiencing our finest hour. Our strength is our togetherness, and this pandemic has pulled us apart, creating a situation where grandparents can't see grandkids, neighbors become strangers, and families are forced to mourn loved ones from afar. This pulling apart of Sioux Falls occurs not only through social distancing but with the way we treat each other and square off in factions, allowing our frustration to carry the day. We have seen evidence of those factions in this room tonight. In my estimation, the best way to cut through this division is with strong leadership, especially in dangerous times. I grew up regarding politicians as courageous souls who would do the right thing regardless of whether it was popular, and I'd like to believe those ideals still exist in some circles of our political world. I haven't seen much of that courage at the state level in South Dakota, and I think that's a shame. Because the worst thing someone could tell themselves looking back on this year is that they played it safe and sat idle when it was time to stand tall and lead. For those reasons, and because the preponderance of data supports the use of face coverings in public, I vote yes on this mandate, which now becomes law."

The outburst of anger that followed was impressive even in the context of all that had occurred, with zealots springing from their chairs to raise fists and surge toward the platform, where councilors gathered materials and headed for the exit, attended by police officers serving as sentinels. Harper didn't want to make it look like an outright escape, so he stood for a moment to face his detractors, failing to consider that his masked visage would fuel their rage. As he finally left the chambers, headed to a back room to face the media, I could see Cap Hawkins observing his movements with the interest of someone who sees defeat as opportunity, knowing the real battle is still to be waged.

NINE

Catholic Central was a tough place to play. The school's campus bordered a busy intersection on the city's west side, making traffic troublesome and parking an adventure. The football stadium featured modern and spacious seating on the home side but rickety bleachers for visitors, creating an air of discomfort that seemed part of the plan. Even with Covid-related attendance rules – two family members per participant, masks required – the visitors' side was nearly full when Connie and I arrived for Edison's much-awaited showdown with the Crusaders. The rattle of a drum line drowned out traffic and knotted my nerves. Catholic Central had a reputation for no-nonsense football embodied by veteran coach Sid Ackman, whose wishbone offense was dismissed as outdated by new-era strategists until they were required to stop it. The Crusaders had captured nine state titles over the past 25 years and were determined to win another. Edison stood in their way, with an undefeated regular season and top playoff seed on the line. "Jeez, how old is their coach?" asked Connie while watching Ackman stalk the field during warmups, clapping his hands furiously. "He's got to be pushing 80," I said. "There are stories about how he forced a kid to play with a broken leg in the state finals one year and then lied about it later. They call him Sid Vicious." We settled in as kickoff approached, watching Edison's cheerleaders rally the crowd with raised pom poms and shrill voices, only to buckle into laughter when one of them missed her cue. It was a sign of things to come for the Nighthawks, who looked out of sorts as Catholic Central barreled down the field on the opening drive for a 7-0 lead. When Edison tried to respond, Brad Hawkins was sacked on a blitz and fumbled, going down in a heap. He contorted his body to try to recover the ball but was struck again by Central defenders, who pounced on the prize and taunted the quarterback, continuing the bad blood that had flared all week.

I watched Hawkins stomp to the sideline and fling his helmet, berating a group of offensive linemen as coaches tried to calm him. They weren't even watching as Central's quarterback faked a handoff and threw to a wide-open receiver for a 14-0 lead just two minutes into the game. "Get your heads out of your ass!" Dale Burgess shouted from a few rows down, a sentiment most parents seemed to share. Edison managed a field goal on the next drive, and the score was still 14-3 late in the first half when I saw Nathan line up wide rather than in the slot, which only happened when they wanted to fool the cornerback for a big gain. Brad dropped back and feigned a short throw, drawing the defender in as Nathan sold the fake and took off at full speed, with Brad lofting the pass just before he was mauled by a linebacker. Connie clutched my shoulder as the ball floated through the lights and landed in our son's hands, only to bounce out after a series of juggles and tumble to the turf. Coach Talley flung his headset as Central fans jeered and Nathan jogged back to the huddle, ignored by most of his teammates. "Get the next one!" someone in the stands shouted, trying to stay positive, but I wished I could reach out onto the field and grab my son, protect him, like I had done for all the years that led to this moment, stretching back to when he was born.

He was delivered a month early and spent time in neonatal intensive care before we could bring him home. The doctors wanted to make sure his lungs were developed enough to allow him to breathe on his own. They set up a rocking chair so Connie could swaddle Nathan for hours, and I would stop by after a night shift at the Gazette, marveling at his weight-lessness, tiny fingers clasping my chest. We brought him home over Christmas and placed his bassinet in the bedroom, where Connie's mother and aunt and their friends entered one by one, as if bearing gifts at the manger. "He's so little!" one of them bellowed after emerging from the room, hand over her heart. "I doubt he'll stay that way," Connie replied curtly, tired of the fuss. The end of the holidays meant facing the reality of being first-time parents in our early 30s, mature enough to raise a child responsibly but rigid enough to feel resentment. Time spent watching a movie, looking up recipes or socializing with friends was now devoted to changing diapers, feeding rituals and round-the-clock soothing, burdens no less arduous for the fact that nearly every new parent experiences them. There were days I'd come home and Connie, frayed from lack of sleep, would thrust the infant toward me and say "here!" as if delivering a parcel, and sometimes that's how it felt. At what point, after all, does a baby become a child? Is there a difference between the resolve to nurture a healthy infant and the emotional spark that fires when he starts moving about, responding to words, beaming back with eyes that mirror your own? And how is that personality influenced? We had moved into a house in central Sioux Falls within walking distance of Nicholls Park, a green expanse of playscapes and gardens filled with sensory proof of a wider world, all from the perspective of a stroller. While Connie was content to be loving toward the boy, cooing and cradling and attending to his needs, I went out and bought "Baby Mozart" CDs and scoured the library for board books, eager to unlock life's mysteries while sheltering him all the same.

My only personal experience with a father-son relationship involved long periods of closeness with my dad and then the shock of hardly seeing him at all. Trying to protect Nathan from the emotional damage I suffered – not to mention the physical trauma of a serious head wound and voyage to the hospital by sea – created a quixotic quest for him not to be hurt at all. Tree climbing was forbidden, especially after the son of a friend tumbled from a brittle branch and nearly broke his neck. Toy guns weren't inherently dangerous but correlated to real-world violence, so they were out as well. When Connie bought Nathan a plastic sword at a medieval festival they attended, I tolerated it for a few days and then found a place to stow it in the attic. Of course, not all calamities could be foreseen.

When he was about five years old, Nathan participated in a Fourth of July parade that allowed kids to decorate their bikes and ride alongside the floats, a procession that started downtown and made its way toward Falls Park, the picturesque city namesake. Connie and I had been speed-walking the route, straining our necks and waving as Nate rode alongside other children, tooting his horn for effect. I had spent days teaching him how to ride, using our front lawn as falling-off point, but he had not yet mastered the art of stopping. I didn't figure that to be a problem in a slow-moving parade until I recalled the downward slope that approached the park, leading past the entrance and toward an intersection. While the other children hit the brakes near the entrance and were met by parents or volunteers, Nathan went speeding past, oblivious to the peril and still sounding his horn. Connie and I initiated our version of emergency mode, blaming each other for the impending catastrophe. "I thought you said he could stop!" she screamed as I sprinted to head him off. "You didn't tell me about this damn hill!" I shouted back, drawing stares from picnickers. By the time I reached Nathan he had passed the old Starlight Bar, where slaughterhouse workers got their fill, and was 20 yards from the intersection before police officers responding to the commotion slowed his roll. "He hasn't learned stopping yet!" I explained weakly, almost out of breath, as Nathan took off his helmet and asked for his mom.

I discovered a series of condensed classics – *Treasure Island, Gulliver's Travels, Black Beauty* – that I read to him at bedtime, pleased when he asked for another chapter. Manners were enforced, to the point where I was militant

about him saying "please" and "thank you" in the most
banal of settings, making sure it stuck. My mother, who
had used the same approach with Wayne and me, remarked
upon Nathan's etiquette when she visited from Michigan,
hinting that perhaps her precedent played a role. "Someone
has to teach kids that," she said to Connie, who rolled her
eyes and changed the subject. My wife envisioned childhood as impulsive and freewheeling, like her own experience. She wanted Nathan to discover his surroundings,
buoyed by parental support, and determine which paths to
explore, while I was in favor of drawing the map. The right
approach was probably somewhere in between, bracketed
by circumstances beyond our control. One summer weekend when I was working, Connie took Nathan to a friend's
lake cabin to swim for the day and was making lunch when
she heard screaming out by the water. From what I was
told, Nathan was climbing beneath the dock and ripped his
hand open on a sharp edge, leaving deep gashes in his palm.
They had to rush him to the nearest clinic for stitches, with
Connie attempting to calm him as he howled in the back
of the car, surrounded by blood-soaked towels. He wore a
bandage for several weeks, curtailing summer activities
and ending his Little League baseball season. "Were you
watching him?" I screamed at Connie that night. "What
if he was drowning? What would have happened then?"
She pointed out that a group of older kids was around and
that it was a fluke accident, tears gathering in her eyes.
I knew she felt terrible, but I couldn't stop myself from
subjecting her to my theory that most accidents were not
really accidents, citing our Fourth of July debacle as proof.
They were avoidable occurrences stemming from reckless

decisions that put people in position to be harmed, and they could be learned from, if it wasn't too late.

———

I was in a surly mood coaching the first Little League game after the incident, with Nathan bandaged up and cheering from the dugout. We had christened our squad the Wolves, foregoing the name of our sponsor, and Nate exchanged wolf howls with his teammates when they weren't arguing over sunflower seeds or which bat to use. This was before my son became disenchanted with the sport, when he regarded spirited sessions of sky-high pop flies as heaven on earth rather than a reason to leave baseball behind. "If they keep score, we're going to try to win," was my adage, and the boys followed along. Our first game after Nate's injury was against a team we dominated earlier in the season, a loss their coach had not forgotten. "We get to play Murderers' Row again," he grumbled when we met at home plate. "Let's try to make it a fair fight."

When the game started, he celebrated not just every hit for his team but every misfortune for ours, including shouts of glee when a grounder slipped through our shortstop's legs. I should have ignored him but instead I returned fire, shouting "Goodbye!" when an opposing player was thrown out at first. In the next inning, when one of their kids flung his bat and almost hit our catcher in the head, I argued that the batter should be declared out, as laid out in league rules. "I need you to settle down, sir," said the umpire, a scrawny high schooler reveling in his authority. When I mentioned protecting players, he stood on his toes to look me in the eye and said, "What does the back of my shirt say, sir?" Given the context of the question, I assumed that it said "Umpire" or "Official," but because he was facing me, there was no way of knowing, and his coltish aggression was infuriating. "I don't know what it says – maybe 'idiot?'" I offered, after which he wheeled around and tossed me from the game. I naturally thought of my father – *My god, am I him?* – as I walked out of the complex and drove to a hill overlooking the diamonds, where I watched the newly inspired Wolves tear their opponent to shreds. I had returned to the field to pick up Nathan after the game when we ran into the opposing coach in the parking lot. "Are you calmed down?" he asked with a smirk. "Now that we kicked your ass again? Yeah, I'm good," I said, watching him fail to muster a response.

Nathan retold that story for years as we drove to baseball and later flag football with his friends, hesitating before "ass" each time and using "A" instead, exhibiting more decorum than his father. The best times were when it was just the two of us in the car, on our way to practices or games and strategizing about the task ahead, not a wistful form of happiness but one to savor in real time, the journey being the thing. "Is this Lil Wayne?" I'd ask as high school musical tastes shifted to rap. "Nice try, Dad...it's Lil Baby." It was a way to replicate the physical closeness we shared when he was younger, when Connie would come downstairs while we watched football and laugh about how Nathan sat so close to me that his body melded into mine, our Detroit Lions jerseys becoming one. When boys grow older, much of that physical connection with fathers is lost, save for ceremonial hugs. Not so for Connie, a round-the-clock embracer who would wrap Nathan in her arms for no apparent reason, in the middle of the kitchen or in front of his friends, while he stood chagrined but not trying to escape. I thought of those annual first days of school when he was an elementary student, smaller than the other kids, curly blond hair a gift from his mom. He'd dress in a collared shirt and khaki shorts that Connie picked out, posing for endless pictures on the playground as teachers with frantic smiles corralled students into orderly lines. Where was the child who smiled for those photos so dutifully, without embarrassment, with something like pride, and would he ever return? When Nathan approached me about messages he received from Brad Hawkins, urging him to go out for the team, my first instinct was to recall his disastrous third-grade tackle football experience and all those articles I had read, and sometimes wrote, about the threat of concussions. The whole thing seemed sudden since there had been no discussions about him playing as a freshman or sophomore. What if he wasn't good enough? What if he got hurt? Of course, there were other considerations, such as making my son happy and giving him a sense of striving for something, belonging to a team, maybe reclaiming some of our lost connections. Is it living vicariously through your child to want to see them succeed in worthy endeavors, to take pride in performance, even as those achievements reflect upon you, repairing things that are broken?

Surely the boy wasn't so fragile that dreams should remain dormant in that wider world to which he was introduced. "Is this football thing for you or your dad?" Connie asked him when the topic came up during dinner. "This is for me," he responded, and we accepted it as truth.

A heavy-hitting halftime speech from Coach Talley – "challenging the manhood of boys," he later told our reporter – energized the Nighthawks. Running plays that worked for Catholic Central in the first half were suddenly going backwards, frustrating their veteran coach and forcing them to throw. When Edison's Taven Robinson picked off a misguided pass and ran it back 60 yards for a touchdown to cut the lead to 14-10, the visitors' bleachers rocked with emotion as Connie screamed into my ear. The teams exchanged touchdowns to make it 21-17 late in the fourth quarter, when Edison's defense rose to the occasion and forced a Crusader punt. Cap Hawkins had been hovering near the sideline for most of the second half, shouting instructions to his son, who now took the field with a chance to keep Edison undefeated and seal the top seed for the playoffs. He appeared to rally his teammates in the huddle rather than berate them, and they blocked with renewed vigor, freeing him up for several long runs into Central territory. The time for trash talking was over. This was about football. Sid Ackman sensed as much and shouted into his headset on the far sideline, desperate to stem the tide. On the next snap, Brad looked ready to take off again with the football, but his path was blocked and he wheeled around behind the line of scrimmage, looking for somewhere to throw. Out of the corner of my eye I saw Nathan's No. 80 jersey streaking across the field, free of defenders with most of the Crusaders worried about Hawkins. The pass hit Nate in the chest and he hung on this time, turning up field and churning his legs before being pushed out inside the 5-yard line, where Brad ran up to help him up and give him a slap on the side of the helmet. Connie and I were speechless, but Dale Burgess shouted, "Hell of a play!" and then watched as his son took a handoff and dove into the end zone for a 24-21 victory that ignited the Edison sideline, with cheerleaders forgetting about the crowd and celebrating amongst themselves, leaping and yelping in unison. Cap weaved around them and pumped his fist toward Dale and the other dads, yelling something about "championship or bust." I searched for Nathan and saw him surrounded by teammates, gesturing excitedly as they pounded on his shoulder pads and patted his back. They all gathered around Coach Talley and let out a roar before running with raised arms to the locker room, resplendent under stadium lights.

TEN

"Rooster!"

The call cut through raw October air, startling me to action. Cap Hawkins and his cohorts had trampled through matted grass and shrunken stalks trying to flush a pheasant for me to shoot, and the time was at hand. I fumbled with the shotgun I had been given and switched off the safety, firing a blast that missed the bird by inches. The recoil sent flashes of pain through my trigger finger. "Fire again!" Cap shouted, but I was too busy shaking my hand and wondering whether I broke my knuckle. He turned his weapon upward before cursing and lowering the barrel. The prize had fluttered out of range. Cap's black Labrador, Bandit, romped toward me before catching my defeated gaze and retreating. The rest of the group tried to stay upbeat. I had agreed to go hunting with Cap and a few of his buddies to learn more about the F.A.R. activist group for a possible Gazette story, especially in the wake of Harper's policy moves. I convinced myself that my lack of experience with pheasant hunting – which lured sportsmen to South Dakota from around the country, filling

up airports, lodges and pop-up strip joints to the tune of
$200 million annually – was a gaping hole on my journalistic
resume.

"Well, it's perfect for social distancing...not that these
guys are worried about that," shrugged Gina when I told her
and Cummings about my plans. Cummings asked if the group
knew we were doing research on them and I had to admit
that it hadn't come up. Things were moving pretty fast. Cap
had floated the invitation after the Catholic Central game,
saying a few of the Edison dads planned on hunting land near
Mitchell, a good way to let off steam before the playoffs. He
had done a nice job on my mower and not charged me much,
and it didn't feel right to turn him down. Of course, even
with my news-gathering motives, I was relieved to hear that
Ed would not make the trip. My interaction with him and his
son had not been pleasant. "Just be careful," said Cummings,
who offered some basic hunting tips and showed me how to
obtain a license. "You'll be a novice out there, and you still
don't know much about this Cap guy, other than he's good
at cleaning out carburetors."

We met in a parking lot across from the Gazette and
piled into Cap's truck, with Bandit in the back. Riding along
was Rick Schumacher, father to Edison's best and largest
offensive lineman, one of the few men in town who could
make Cap appear normal-sized. "Remind me not to piss this
guy off today," said Cap, who wore a brown hunting jacket
and serious expression, his complexion ruddy in daylight. He
told us that a family friend had a tract of land he was permitted to use as long as certain rules were followed, among them
no consumption of alcohol during the hunt. "That's what
they call driving a hard bargain," said Rick, whose hulking

frame jostled me as he enjoyed his own joke. Cap assured us that he had a few beers in the cooler for when the shooting was done. He struck a somber presence behind the wheel, making occasional observations but mainly content to soak up rural landscapes and the wordless stories they told. The weather was overcast and windy, which would make it diffi-cult for Bandit to get the scent of pheasants on the ground. "It'll be a bit of a battle today," said Cap, looking back at his dog to the extent that it wasn't clear who he was addressing. "There are some pretty good spots near the Jim River that we'll take a look at...I'm guessing there are some birds down there." Rick asked him if the Jim River was the same as the James River, which got Cap to chuckling again, released from his earlier reverie. "One and the same, my friend," he said. "One and the same."

When we pulled off the interstate and reached harvested fields, Bandit became more restless, yowling at the familiar feel of gravel roads. "Quiet down now!" said Cap, pulling into a clearing where two men in hunter orange stood outside their truck. One was Cap's cousin, we learned, and the other worked a nearby farm. They both regarded my Gazette-branded fleece jacket and jeans with suspicion. "Better get these boys some vests," said Cap, gesturing at Rick and myself. "One's a newspaperman, which speaks for itself. The other's so big I'm worried someone might shoot him out of fear." He walked me through how to load shells into a 12-gauge and reviewed the essentials of carrying, aiming and firing. Clouds were dense and the gusts had increased, providing a gloomy backdrop as we entered the field. Cap grumbled that we didn't have blockers at the other end of the property to contain birds, allowing pheasants to flock to freedom. He said something to his cousin about bringing more guys next time. Bandit bounded about unperturbed, working to flush birds as we walked in formation. I was so engrossed with the ritual that I missed our first shot. The dog had sent a rooster fluttering above us at high speed, and Cap was the first to respond. He raised and sighted his weapon in one fluid motion and fired. *Click*. In his haste to hand out shells to the rest of the group and make sure my double-barrel was loaded, he had neglected to get ammunition in his chamber, a mistake that sparked a torrent of profanity and some ribbing from his cousin. "Too much time in the city, I guess," he called to Cap, who was rummaging in his vest for shells. "Too much time hanging around you fuckin' guys," Cap muttered.

After about an hour we headed south to an acreage close to the river. The land was uneven but had been stripped down, with fewer places for birds to hide. Cap shifted strategy and sent me down to the end of the property to block while he and the others walked toward me with Bandit, whose spirit had not sagged. I stood there as the others stalked through the field trying to flush birds my way, their voices choppy in gathering winds. At one point their bodies were shielded by a bluff and Cap was the first to emerge, about 50 yards away. I thought maybe he had a shot because he raised his shotgun, but he didn't fire. Instead he slowly lowered the weapon, which to my untrained eye appeared to be pointed directly at my chest. I stood frozen, wondering if I should wave my arms or shout. My heart was pounding when Rick's massive body became visible and Cap raised his shotgun again toward the sky, calling something to the group before marching on. A few minutes later is when I heard the call of "Rooster!" and missed my moment, my knuckle stinging with pain. Cap offered to get me another shotgun, but I shrugged him off as they continued their hunt and bagged a few birds, Rick shouting encouragement as Bandit scurried back with his kill.

We drove back to the original starting point and packed away the guns as Cap passed around some beers. Darker clouds had rolled in, increasing the afternoon chill. Before long, it was just the Edison dads talking about the upcoming playoff game against Yankton, a team the Nighthawks had handled easily during the regular season. "We should beat those guys by 40," said Rick, arching his back against Cap's truck. "What did they have against us last time, maybe 100 total yards? This is like having a bye into the semifinals." Cap laughed and took a swig of his Busch Light. "If your boy can keep Brad clean, he should have an easy time of it," he told Rick. "But there's no use getting overconfident this time of year. Playoff games can get screwy. We need to put Yankton away and not give them life…drain the blood right out of them." It seemed an apt metaphor with a stack of dead birds in our midst. I watched as a utility truck drove slowly past, its driver hazarding a wave. "It sounds like a few schools are having to forfeit playoff games because of Covid issues," I said, noting a story we had run that morning. "Not enough players to field a team." Cap looked at me like I had uttered something unspeakable. "Those are small-town teams that nobody gives a shit about," he said, draining his beer and crushing the can with his boot. He looked at Rick and smiled. "Hell, you lose one kid to the sniffles and you can't field a team at that level, right? The big boys will be fine."

Rick was staying with a friend in Mitchell, so we dropped him off and were headed out of town when Cap pulled into a roadside bar called Teasers that I had heard about but never entered. The marquee was a picture of a naked woman sitting in a cocktail glass. "This is part of the pheasant hunting ritual around here," Cap said after parking the truck, engine still running. "I figured you needed the whole experience to get it right." We could hear music from the low-lying building, where neon accents offset peeling paint. "What about Covid?" I said. "I'm surprised this place is even open." Cap took the keys from the ignition and faced me, eyes fierce in the remaining light. "*What about Covid? What about Covid?*" he sneered. "The girls are wearing fuckin' masks, and you don't have to get near 'em if you don't want to. They're probably carrying around a bunch of shit that's worse than 'rona, if you ask me. Let's just get a drink and tell a few war stories...we'll leave whenever you want."

Men in work shirts and camouflage sat and sipped their drinks, furtively watching the action. There was a bar along the wall with a group of college kids talking loudly, trying to impress a masked strawberry blonde with her legs crossed, wearing a G-string that showed her slight belly. She had pasties on her nipples, in accordance with state law. In the middle of the room was a T-shaped stage with colored lights, a stripper pole and up-close seats that Cap called "sniffers' row," with dollar bills stacked like shrines to the sexual fantasies they funded. "Please welcome to the stage the lovely and talented Monique!" the DJ bleated over blurred speakers as a sad-looking brunette took the stage. Cap pointed me toward a table in the back, where a waitress was clearing off bottles. "Hello darlin'!" he said while shedding his jacket and sitting down. "Couple of vodka shots...and burgers and beers. Busch Light OK with you?" I nodded and gazed at the stage, where Monique was spinning languidly to Motley Crue's "Home

Sweet Home," paying little mind to the loners below. Cap snorted at my curiosity and pulled his chair closer to the table so I could hear him over the music.

"I grew up not far from here," he said. "Small cattle ranch near Letcher. I ended up playing football at Mitchell after the coach got wind of someone my size who could move around a bit. 'You need to play real football, not that nine-man shit,' he told me, and my dad was fine with it if the work got done. They arranged it somehow that I could live at home and get up early to help with feeding before high-tailing it to Mitchell to attend classes, or some of them at least." The waitress dropped off our drinks and Cap made a toast to my first pheasant hunt as we downed our shots, the vodka searing my throat. He made a swirling motion with his finger to signal another round. "I was a 6-foot-4, 260-pound defensive end, striking fear in the hearts of quarterbacks, as they say. They named me team captain and everyone started calling me Cap, which sounded better than Harold. Schools like Nebraska and Iowa sent letters, but my dad wasn't sure about me leaving the area. I told him my younger brother, Kyle, would be able to help around the place." When I asked him what his mom thought, he shifted in his seat. "She died when I was in sixth grade, and our family never recovered. Fuckin' breast cancer. Took a strong woman who raised two boys and was active in the community and just whittled her away, day by day. They tried radiation and chemo until it spread to her lungs and then they just made her comfortable at home. By the end, she didn't want me to see her like that, wanted me to remember her like she was. 'Leave me be,' she'd tell Kyle and myself, and we'd be crying outside the room. 'Could be the drugs talking,' the doctors said. 'She's not herself.' The neighbors pitched in to make sure work got done, and my old man sat with her until the minute she died. He never cried, at least that I saw." Cap took a swig of his beer and nodded when the shots and burgers arrived, waiting for the waitress to leave before continuing. "My mom had been one to keep me on the straight and narrow, not with punishment or a hot temper but just by wanting to please her. Dangerous thing when you let other people be your conscience. By the time I got to high school, I was acting out and drinking and my grades went to shit. I had to sit the first two games of my junior year after I beat up a kid and sent him to the hospital. Some of those college coaches must have found out about it because the letters stopped coming. I ended up going to a junior college in Nebraska, where my grades could be overlooked. My dad didn't want me to go, but I told him I wasn't done playing football, even though I knew that Kyle would bear the brunt of me not being there. He was smaller but more athletic than me, a damn fine quarterback and basketball player, and more reliable on the ranch. My dad came to see him as a younger, more promising version of myself."

We downed our second round of shots and the DJ called up another dancer. Cap stared at the table, perhaps wondering how much to reveal. "I came home for Thanksgiving my sophomore year in college and convinced Kyle to sneak out with me to meet some buddies and smoke some weed," he said. "Thought it would do him some good...kid was too uptight and had a lot of pressure on him. I didn't want to wake the old man up by starting that diesel engine, so I told Kyle we'd push the truck away from the house in neutral, with him in back and me at the driver's side door, where I could steer. Biggest mistake of my life. The grass was wet and we were on a slight incline, so we couldn't get any traction and the truck started rolling backward. By the time I reached the brakes, Kyle was pinned against the grain bin by a two-ton truck. The sound still keeps me up at night. His right leg broke when he tried to get up but his left leg was worse, a crushed kneecap that cut off all the blood and had be amputated once he got to Sioux Falls. That time my dad cried." I was feeling the vodka but managed to stammer something about how sorry I was, words he waved off. "I dropped out of college while Kyle was in rehab and worked at a body shop in Sioux Falls," he continued. "Got a girl pregnant and married her, at least for a few years. That's where Brad came from. Kyle learned how to walk on a prosthetic leg and decided to get a nursing degree after high school, figuring farm work wasn't for him. He's in the Denver area and we talk from time to time. From the day my brother left the hospital, though, my father never spoke to me again. Not a fuckin' word. Never set eyes on his grandson. We buried him a few years back and all anyone talked about at the funeral was how much the man loved Kyle, as if I wasn't sitting right there. The only thing I carried from my old man was my devotion to my son and my pride in how he plays football. I thank God that Brad's all in one piece and nobody has fucked things up for him yet, not even me. Anyone who thinks I'm going to let some bullshit virus take away his athletic career has got another thing coming."

A few moments later he was on his feet, saying "Come on, girl" while whisking away a skinny dancer whose milk-white skin speckled with glitter. She was laughing and leaning on him as he whispered in her ear. She looked in my direction for just a second before they disappeared behind the beaded curtains of a VIP room. I could see the silhouette of her body grinding as Axl Rose's voice wailed through the bar: *She's got a smile that it seems to me, reminds me of childhood memories.* I thought back to the night I was kicked out of a strip club in Sioux Falls while attending a bachelor party for one of the Gazette copy editors, who had never had a lap dance in his life. We were trying to remedy that when some leather-jacketed goon sat down at our table, saying he recognized me from the newspaper and asking me if this was where I hung out. "Shouldn't you be out covering a game instead of staring at titties?" he said with a stupid grin. I told him to go fuck himself and hurled my gin and tonic at him from across the table, sending him scattering with an incredulous "Whoa!" that turned some dancers' heads. Before I knew it, the bouncer had me in a headlock and was walking me toward the exit. When I told Connie the story, she said it sounded like a girly way to get kicked out of a titty bar, throwing a drink and all. I promised her I would try to do something more egregious next time. "Oh, I think your gentlemen's club days are over," she had said then, yet here I was proving her wrong in the middle of a pandemic at some second-rate roadhouse, listening to Guns N' Roses.

I got up and threw a few bills on the table, about to head to the parking lot, when someone tapped me on the shoulder and said, "Not leaving, are you?" It was the strawberry blonde from earlier, smiling and rocking on her heels. She pressed her body into mine and brushed her hand across my crotch while looking into my eyes, which were having trouble focusing. "I'm not a buyer tonight," I said, trying to summon the lingo. "This one's on Cap," she countered, leading me past the VIP booth and into a back room that looked like a changing area, where she guided me to the couch before ripping off her mask and pasties. "That's better," she purred, getting down on her knees and stroking my thighs. I tried to say something and stammered, which made her snicker as she got up to writhe in my lap. Her breasts were slippery, a hint of body odor amid the perfume. I could feel the thumping of bass from inside the bar, and the room was spinning. "You like this?" she asked, and in my groggy state I only managed garish, movie-like responses, saying "fuck, yeah" and urging her on. She reached inside my pants to determine my readiness and then she was tugging at my jeans and underwear, crumpling them to the floor. She tore open a condom and performed her task with precision, bobbing her head up and down as I contorted with pleasure, muttering "oh yeah" and "Jesus Christ" until the final spasm, when she stood and threw me a towel. "They don't like it if we stay back here too long," she said, rummaging for her mask. By the time I returned to the bar, Cap was talking animatedly with one of the bouncers. They both smiled at me as I approached and Cap slapped me on the back as we made our way to the parking lot, where Bandit was patiently waiting.

The ride home went fast. My mind was reeling, and I lashed out when he teased me about the back-room encounter. "What the hell was that all about?" I asked, and he laughed and said, "I suppose she tied you up and dragged you into that situation – do you want to file a report?" I told him that wasn't funny, and he tilted his head, as if trying to decide. I said that the only reason I agreed to the hunting trip was to learn about his anti-lockdown group, and I had come up empty. We had barely even talked about Ed. "We can talk about him now if you want," said Cap. "Remember how I told you that I got married – well, Ed is my ex-wife's brother. She moved to Michigan after the divorce and I kept custody of Brad, believe it or not. Tells you what sort of shape she was in. Ed shares a place in Michigan with her, but he and Eddie still make it back to South Dakota now and then, especially now with the mayor's bullshit. I'm focused on Harper not fucking up our football season, but Ed has bigger concerns. He's seen a lot of damage done in Michigan and has tried to fight against it. He sees these restrictions as taking away people's constitutional freedoms, and he doesn't mess around. It might be wise for you to talk some sense in your buddy Harper, either personally or with one of your blistering editorials."

That sounded like a threat, and I told him so. His silence seemed to confirm it. By that time we were in Sioux Falls and pulling into the parking lot, where my car was waiting. I decided to bring up that moment during the hunt when it looked like he had his shotgun pointed at me, only to pull it away. Cap pondered it for a moment and then grabbed my wrist as I was getting ready to leave. "When I decide to point a gun at you," he said to me, "you'll know it."

ELEVEN

Governor Lawton's political bargain was becoming more complex. President Trump contracted Covid in early October and spent several days at Walter Reed Hospital, making it tougher for his supporters to claim the virus was a hoax fueled by media and Democrats. With the presidential election just weeks away and Trump not able to hold rallies, pressure mounted on surrogates such as Lawton to make the case for another term. There was no escaping pandemic response as a key issue – especially with hospitalizations and deaths surging again in the Upper Midwest. Republican governors of North Dakota and Iowa reversed their hands-off approach and enacted mask policies in their states, but Lawton refused to budge. She enhanced her national MAGA profile while taking political hits at home, with South Dakota ranked among the top 10 states in per capita Covid deaths. The talking point among her critics was that she cared more about a far-flung version of freedom than guarding against the virus. We published a story revealing that Lawton's team was furious at Mayor Harper for calling her bluff and pushing through a Sioux Falls mask mandate, assuming the role of take-charge executive that she relinquished. "They're concerned that he's positioning himself as a white knight who can draw enough moderate and independent votes to unseat her in 2022, becoming the first Democratic governor elected in South Dakota since 1974," the article read. "Sources say that Lawton has alienated just enough establishment Republicans to make it a possibility."

So it was not a cheerful governor who appeared at a manufacturing plant in Aberdeen, Harper's hometown, to help announce a federal grant for expanded production of respirator masks, an ironic juxtaposition not lost on those in attendance. The state's two U.S. senators and lone congressional representative, all Republicans, sported face coverings while sitting in folding chairs in the parking lot, awaiting their turn to speak. Lawton positioned herself a few feet away, Ray-Bans her only facial accessory. Gina had sent Patrick to cover the event at the last minute, and I watched the livestream from my home office, still reeling a few days after my hunting trip. I could see Norah Newcombe working the parking lot like a spin room, chatting up reporters and aides. Every few minutes she would walk over and say something into Lawton's ear, drawing an obligatory nod. She also spent a lot of time talking to a maskless man that I recognized as Peter Rasmussen, CEO of Sawyer Health in Sioux Falls. He was thinner than I remembered, almost gaunt in the face, but still managed a certain elegance as he glided between politicians and plant executives. "Why the hell is Rasmussen there?" I messaged Gina, who responded quickly: "No idea... maybe because there are cameras?"

Rasmussen had made the most of media appearances

since arriving in Sioux Falls from Ohio in the mid-1990s, with much to boast about. He took the reins of a provincial hospital and turned it into a regional powerhouse by focusing on fundraising, acquisitions and branding. His biggest move was to nurture a relationship with credit card magnate Teddy Sawyer, crafting a deal to make him the system's namesake – and build multiple statues in his honor – in exchange for a donation of $300 million. To considerable fanfare, the duo announced that a portion of the money would be devoted to curing a major disease, which they unveiled with considerable gusto to be childhood lupus. It was a clever PR gambit that boiled the exceedingly complex discipline of molecular biology down to game-show theatrics, and it was all Rasmussen. He was a master at hospital administration and marketing, but the medical component eluded him. He knew how to wow people, not heal them.

We first met when I was researching a story about college recruiting and traveled with Sioux Falls' top AAU basketball squad to a tournament in Omaha. Rasmussen, whose son was on the team, introduced himself with the ease of someone who formed alliances for a living. He grew up in suburban Cleveland but adapted to South Dakota sensibilities by wearing cowboy boots and driving a pickup truck, which one of our readers pointed out listed at $65,000, eroding its everyman allure. "What do you think of this facility?" he asked me that day at the basketball tournament. "Could be a lot better, right? The bathroom smells like piss and the hot dogs are cold. There's no place for parents to sit and unwind, maybe have a beer. And they need more courts, better access. If you're going to ask parents to spend large chunks of time in these venues, why not do it right?" He was not asking my opinion as much as plotting his next move. About a year later, Sawyer Health purchased land north of Sioux Falls to build a sprawling youth sports complex, with an orthopedic component that guaranteed referrals for broken ankles and twisted knees.

That spirit of innovation served Rasmussen well but rubbed some the wrong way, including doctors who found his focus on personal publicity and pet projects unseemly. He had detractors on the board of directors even before the pandemic hit, but Covid hastened his fall. Taking cues from the Lawton administration, Sawyer Health was slow to respond to the crisis and made questionable policy moves, including signing on to a hydroxychloroquine trial that pleased Trump's White House but raised questions about political agendas. The trial was cut short as research on the malaria drug fizzled elsewhere. Those expecting robust leadership from South Dakota's largest hospital in the early stages of a public health crisis were largely disappointed, including the Sawyer Health board, which explored a merger with a hospital in Colorado that would set the stage for a new CEO, with no cure for childhood lupus forthcoming.

After a series of canned speeches in Aberdeen, Lawton agreed to an impromptu press conference in a corner of the lot. As Patrick scrambled to establish his livestream amid the bustle of TV reporters, a passing motorist honked and shouted "USA!" before peeling out at the intersection. "Another satisfied customer," deadpanned Newcombe, who then ridiculed a reporter for asking whether the governor would restrict indoor dining or curtail public gatherings with cases on the rise. "Does anyone have a serious question?" she asked, "or are we just going to play games today?" Lawton motioned for her to cool it and took over, launching into her boilerplate speech on personal responsibility and trusting South Dakotans to make the right decisions, as opposed to those running liberal states. "Why don't you talk about governors who ordered people to shelter in place as businesses, schools and churches were shuttered?" Lawton asked reporters. "We're only beginning to understand the financial and emotional toll that these draconian measures have inflicted upon everyday Americans, and I think that's a shame." Patrick jumped in with a question about masks, asking why Lawton didn't wear a face covering like other public officials at the event. Did she disagree with national health experts about the efficacy of masks? "I'm here because as governor I'm supporting a local business that is making a difference during a challenging time for our country," she said. "I've said all along that people who want to wear a mask should do so. But this whole idea of forcing people to wear them, or shaming people when they don't, that's just wrong. I don't think that's what government should be about."

"The city of Sioux Falls apparently disagrees with you," countered Patrick. "The mask mandate has taken effect and people are following it, by and large."

Lawton lowered her sunglasses as if to get a better look at who asked the question, and Newcombe cleared her throat. If the governor planned to go on the offensive publicly against Harper, her in-state political nemesis, this was the moment. I reminded myself to thank Gina for sending a reporter.

"My responsibility is to the entirety of South Dakota, not just Sioux Falls," Lawton began. "And I disagree with your assertion that the 'city of Sioux Falls' disagrees with me, as opposed to certain people. I find it unfortunate that Mayor Harper has decided to follow in the radical footsteps of Democrat mayors across America as a means of pursuing his political agenda."

"And what political agenda is that?" Patrick asked.

"The agenda of trying to challenge the Republican rule of a duly elected governor in a state that cherishes freedom," said Lawton. "Mr. Harper is new to politics, as you know, and doesn't understand how things work. He has chosen to agree with me privately and clash with me publicly, probably because he sees himself in my role someday. I'm here to tell you that's another case where he will fall on the wrong side of history."

Newcombe leaned in to stop the line of questioning, gesturing toward a TV reporter to change the subject, but Patrick was too quick for her.

"Is this only about the mask mandate?" he asked. "It seems like there's more going on behind the scenes."

"You have to know these people," Lawton sneered. "Mask mandates only scratch the surface. They will gradually erode your rights because they think you can't take care of yourself and your family. I happen to know that the esteemed mayor is considering shutting down in-person school in Sioux Falls, which I think would be a disaster for the largest district in the state and the students who desire a proper education. I hope he has a change of heart."

I stared at the screen, trying to make sure I heard her right. How many people had Harper told that he was weighing that option, other than myself? It couldn't have been many. So how did Lawton know? And why was she airing it publicly? Maybe she was trying to mobilize opposition after misreading the mask mandate process. Regardless of her motives, it was clear to me that no in-person school meant no football, which would force Edison out of the playoffs. As I pondered that scenario, I heard Lawton introduce Rasmussen and thank Sawyer Health for supporting her in-state leadership during the pandemic. A message popped up from Gina: "Did she just claim a political endorsement from a non-profit health system?" I responded with a familiar refrain: "Welcome to 2020."

Rasmussen turned on the charm, talking about how welcoming the Aberdeen community had been. He praised Lawton's leadership "during this long and painful crisis" and thanked her for working with Sawyer Health to meet the demands of the moment.

"Why aren't you wearing a mask, sir?" a TV reporter asked.

"Well, to be perfectly honest, I have had Covid," Rasmussen responded. "I wasn't as careful as I should have been and socialized a bit – some of it for my job, of course – and ended up feeling terrible for a couple weeks. This virus is the real deal, I can tell you that. I'll bet I lost 20 pounds. But now I'm back and I've got the all-clear from our doctors, as well as plenty of antibodies. I could wear a mask, sure, but it would be merely symbolic, and I'm not interested in symbolism, especially if it curtails freedom. I sent a letter to employees today to explain my position on that. I believe President Trump had a similar approach after he was infected and got better." Newcombe stepped in to end the press conference – "nothing more to see here, people" – as Rasmussen tucked notes into his vest pocket, blind to the turn of events. Gina sent me a bunch of skull emojis to state the obvious: Rasmussen's stint at Sawyer Health was over. He resigned a few hours later, forced out by the board, which handed the interim job to the chief financial officer and reiterated the importance of mask-wearing as a CDC recommendation and the official stance of the health system, with no mention of Lawton.

I waited until Patrick's story was edited and posted before jumping on Twitter, linking to our coverage and adding my own comment: "Anatomy of a disaster." I had about 10,000 followers, a decent amount for a paper the size of the Gazette, and as usual there were a flurry of responses, about 50/50 for and against the tone of Rasmussen's remarks. One of the first tweets that caught my eye said, "What exactly was wrong with what he or the governor said? Maybe the Gazette can stop lying and answer that question." I glanced at the profile photo, which was somewhat grainy and poorly cropped but unmistakably that of my father.

I knew about my dad's pro-Trump proclivities from posts on Facebook, but my interest in that site had waned. The pandemic turned Facebook, from my experience, into a morass of misinformation and acrimony, where copy-and-paste conclusions on masks or Anthony Fauci or vaccines tore friendships and families asunder. The phenomenon of knowing where everyone stands on everything is overrated, as Connie discovered when her cousin in California, she of the annual Christmas cards and birthday barrages, called Connie out for criticizing Trump's Covid response and vowed to never speak to her again. Not a devastating development, I assured my wife, but surely a sign of the times, even at the Gazette. Early in the pandemic, several reporters lashed out at editorials we wrote critical of Lawton's refusal to issue stay-at-home orders, straining the traditional divide between edit board and newsroom. Gina and I were shocked when our female entertainment reporter, not long out of college with a peppy writing style, started railing in a Zoom meeting about how lockdowns were tyrannical and we should just brace for herd immunity, leading some staffers to nod and others to tinker with their keyboard. "Well, that's a viewpoint," I told her patiently. "You're entitled to it, although I might suggest more research on the science behind herd immunity. As I've noted before, please don't share such views on social media because you're representing the Daily Gazette and we want to maintain objectivity on these matters."

That was straight from corporate policy, with opinion writers the exception, and it was getting harder to hold the line. Readers and activists lashed out at journalists for not doing enough to fight back against Lawton or, from the other side, engaging in "scare mongering" on the Covid threat. There were days when Twitter discourse eclipsed the news operation in terms of eyeballs and energy, an alarming development to someone whose career kicked off before social media or even the internet, when readers were more removed but no less invested. A few years after I arrived in Sioux Falls, I was at the grocery store when a well-dressed woman stopped and asked if I was the sports reporter from the

Gazette. I acknowledged that I was and she moved forward to embrace me, purse dangling awkwardly from her arm, as shoppers stared. A few months earlier I had spoken to her on the phone for a story about her sixth-grade son, born without a left arm, who played basketball for his school and gained confidence from those efforts. The article explained how the woman and her husband felt pride at the birth of their son but were understandably shocked to learn that he wasn't perfect, in a biological sense. After running through all the ways that the boy enjoyed a normal life, with basketball a part of that acceptance, I ended the story with a line about his parents watching him play and how the "couple is bursting with pride." She told me how much those words had uplifted her son and their family and then resumed shopping, leaving behind a feeling that likes or retweets can't convey, a reminder of what the work is for.

By the time I had a chance to call my dad to discuss his Aberdeen-related Twitter response, warm reminiscence had been replaced by rancor. He was two years into his fourth marriage and had purchased a country estate in South Carolina so wife Cynthia, a former aerobics instructor 30 years his junior, could manage their horses. I was reminding myself not to reference these equestrian pursuits when he answered the phone and said, "Ah, the intrepid reporter, all the way from South Dakota. Let me guess...you're calling to silence me, right?"

    I ran through a mental checklist of calming techniques

before responding. "No one's silencing anybody, Dad. I just want you to show me some respect and not try to embarrass me on Twitter. I'm not going to respond to you publicly, so what's the point?"

"What's the point, he says. That's beautiful. What's the point of sticking up for a hospital guy who lost his job because he said something that makes total sense. He had the coronavirus – whatever that is, really – and now he's immune so he's not going to wear a mask. And you guys butcher him to the point where he gets tossed out into the street like some bum. Maybe that's the point."

I could hear Cynthia in the background chirping away, something about antibodies and screwing the CDC. I pretended not to hear her. Stay focused, I told myself.

"Peter Rasmussen is going to be just fine," I said. "He's got a golden parachute of more than a million bucks and was on his way out before today. This just sealed it. The larger issue is that I'm trying to run a newspaper at a difficult time, and it's not helpful to have my own father taking shots at our coverage and accusing us of lying."

He chuckled at that. "I forgot how sensitive you are – not exactly Ben Bradlee I'm dealing with here. Hey, hold on a minute." While he went back and forth with Cynthia about a crisis in the kitchen, something about the garbage disposal, I considered probing why he still lionized Bradlee's Washington Post tenure while attacking today's journalists as fake news, figuring nostalgia would be the most generous explanation.

"So how's my grandson doing in football?" he said.

"You mean Nathan? He has a name, you know. You'd be better acquainted with him if you came to visit. You haven't been out here since Connie and I were married."

"You're telling me things I already know," he said. "We can't really go anywhere with these horses to take care of, and God knows we can't travel with the Covid stuff going on – at least that's what your newspaper keeps telling people. So what's the football update? He's playing flanker?"

"They don't call it that anymore, but yes," I told him. "He was a pretty good flag football player, and a group of seniors found out about him and recruited him over the summer to play wide receiver. The team is one of the best in the state – they play in the quarterfinals next week."

I thought he might ask for more information, like Edison's opponent or when they play, but he turned the conversation back to himself and his golf game, another reason he and Cynthia migrated south.

"I shot my age the other day," he told me. "Only two bogeys on the back nine. The guys I play with pitched in and got me a plaque, called it the Old Geezer Award or something like that. Great guys, really, despite their southern accents. But you probably don't want to hear about my outdoor excursions while you're cooped up all day with your job."

I told him how we were still working from home, how some days you didn't even feel like a journalist. You're a frequenter of Zoom meetings who answers emails and deflects social media madness. You wake up and think about what needs to be posted online, what didn't get done the night before, and make sure you don't miss anything in the day ahead – daily coronavirus numbers, health department updates, questions about testing. All coronavirus, all the time. Advertisers were dropping and a new round of buyouts were coming, but I didn't tell him that. He had enough ammunition for media bashing already.

"Sounds like you've got a lot on your plate," he offered, a sign he was ready to hang up. Cynthia was scolding someone, probably their dog, in the background. My dad shushed her and said, "I'll tell you what – I'm still going to comment on Twitter, but I won't go after your coverage, OK? You guys are fine. I'll save my venom for CNN."

———

In the editors meeting the next morning, we talked about repackaging our coverage from Aberdeen and looking for follow-ups, such as what new leadership would mean for Sawyer Health. "I'll have somebody put together a timeline of Rasmussen's stint in Sioux Falls – there's plenty of stuff in the archives," said Gina. We noted how Rasmussen's demise stole the thunder from the governor's comments about Harper, which would have been the lead story any other day. "She's basically going to war with the mayor of Sioux Falls, calling him a radical leftist and a political novice who's angling for her job," said Cummings, munching on an energy bar. "I'd say that merits a bit of second-day analysis." I told him Patrick could handle that and we should make it our 1A centerpiece, with the Rasmussen follow as secondary. Harper had declined comment on Lawton's remarks the night before, but things could change. "How about your hunting experience?" asked Cummings, who already knew that I failed to bag a pheasant. I hadn't told him, or anyone, about the trip to Teasers. "Are we going to get a story about that F.A.R. group this week?" he said. "What's going on with those guys?" I told him that I was still working on it and a few of the key members had skipped the trip. I was concerned about giving a fringe activist group more publicity than it deserved, and I figured Cap would lean on me if he knew we were planning a story. Besides, there were other things to write about. "I'm thinking about putting together an editorial about how schools should stay open, even with cases rising a bit," I told Gina and Cummings. "I know there are concerns with community spread, but remote learning was a disaster last spring and I think Harper is on the wrong track if he's pursuing this. We need to balance the concerns about Covid with the needs of students and their families, which means government backing off."

There was silence for a moment, and I thought that maybe I had muted myself and they hadn't heard me. Cummings had stopped chewing and finally leaned in to speak.

"This is a bit of a departure for you," he said. "Are you feeling all right?"

"Of course," I said, but it wasn't very convincing. The truth was that I felt like hell.

TWELVE

My heart pounded as I lolled in bed, the literal thump-thump of blood pumping through arteries, body swaddled in sweat. Sleep was a broken promise. Maybe it's just anxiety, I told myself. But when I left the covers to go to the bathroom, chills rolled through me like a current, an immune system on high alert. How could I have been so stupid? It was five days since the hunting trip, the standard incubation period for Covid, and it felt like I had begged to get infected. After months of being cautious, high-mindedly so, admonishing others for ignoring guidelines, I allowed myself to be placed in dangerous settings, including a goddamned strip joint. This went beyond having dinner in a restaurant or forgetting my mask at the hardware store. This was craven and reckless. Guilt burned through me like fever, cluttering my thoughts.

If I were tested and found positive, Nathan would be deemed a close contact and forced to quarantine for two weeks, essentially ending his football season. I didn't say anything to him that morning when I made his lunch for

school. We talked about what time he had practice that afternoon and discussed the upcoming Yankton game. "Nice look,"
he said on the way out, and I glanced at the mirror to see my
hair twisted in tangents from the rough night. I fooled myself
into thinking that maybe I had a case of the flu. There was
no sore throat or cough, after all, and I still had a sense of
smell. That morning I walked through the house engaging
in various scent tests, inhaling a jar of peanut butter or one
of Connie's candles or her nail polish remover, which burned
my nostrils. The next day, I felt worse, weighed down by a
sweet, sticky fatigue that clouded my head and made the
most basic of tasks bothersome. I reached into the kitchen
cupboard and pulled out the jar of peanut butter, twisted it
open and took a deep whiff, desperate for a familiar aroma
that never arrived.

That afternoon I got a text from Nathan: "I think I
might have Covid. I can't taste anything." When I didn't
answer immediately, he followed up: "I don't feel sick or
anything. Just kinda scared." That last part hit me. Assuming
he caught it from me, I had managed to drag my kid into this
mess, jeopardizing his health and status at school. It was also
getting tougher for me to fake my way through work. Stories
sent to me for editing or headlines sat idle in my queue,
leading to the inevitable Slack message: "Close?" or "ETA
on that one?" I finally informed Gina that I had a migraine,
which wasn't true, and that I needed to lie down for a while.
She said she would cover for me, but how long could that
last? The election was the following week, with legislative
races and ballot measures and a presidential contest in which
South Dakota's governor was politically invested. There was
no time to be sick. I cornered Nathan in the basement that

night while Connie was making dinner. I decided that I would fight through it and not tell him that I most likely had Covid, and I counseled him to keep his own case quiet unless he started feeling ill. He told me that several of his teammates, including Brad, had talked openly about not being able to taste or smell – symptoms they kept silent for fear of being pulled out of school and off the football field. Others had more severe cases and were too fatigued to carry out the ruse, but for most the plan was to avoid disclosure until the playoffs were over.

"This is not just at Edison," Nate told me. "I've heard of coaches at other schools telling kids not to get tested because they'll be out for at least two games, maybe more, and their close contacts could also be gone. Better to keep it in the clubhouse." He said it casually, having adopted the jargon, but there was an edge in his voice. After all this time of hearing how coronavirus was leading to hospitalizations and deaths, shutting down the economy and shattering lives, it was quite likely that he had been infected, and he would go it alone. We knew that his mother would push for him to get tested, and we had come too far with our football experience to have it end that way. I cautioned him not to tell his friends or teammates, because all it took was one to inform a teacher or principal and ruin everything. I hated how that sounded as soon as I said it. I was now hiding my symptoms from my family and co-workers while pulling my son into a duplicitous pact to keep his school and mother in the dark, all while lecturing government officials about their lack of vigilance in keeping the virus from spreading. I could have put my foot down and told Nathan that there were more important things than football, that we needed to make sacrifices to protect others from the spread of illness, but that didn't happen. I simply nodded at him when we were called to dinner and put my hand on his shoulder as we walked up the stairs, a gesture more calculating than tender.

———————

The situation with Connie was more complicated. She had been sick for a period over the summer and later told me that she thought she might have had Covid, a suspicion that led her to take a week off from her pharmaceutical sales job and go to bed early each night, citing a headache. Her decision to steer clear of us rather than get tested was a curious one for her, perhaps motivated by wanting to maintain a sliver of normalcy at a time when such a goal seemed attainable, before cases started spiking again in the fall. At any rate, keeping her distance (and keeping mine) was made possible by separate bedrooms, a staple of our relationship since Nathan's post-toddler years, when my snoring, combined with the decline in physical intimacy that showed no signs of reversal, made such accommodations practical. It was not a situation that Connie accepted readily. She shared a childhood memory of playing at a friend's house and learning that the girl's parents slept in separate rooms, a revelation that seemed scandalous to her young ears, the marriage irredeemable. "I don't want to be that couple," she told me.

She scheduled appointments with a marriage counselor, a woman in her 30s named Stephanie whose stone-and-steel office suite seemed more suited to commercial real estate. At our first session, she cautioned Connie about making absolute statements such as "You never want to do anything with me!" or "I always have to initiate!" – noting that such proclamations are typically exaggerated and make a partner defensive. "That just causes him to shut down," said Stephanie, who wore turtlenecks and wool skirts and wielded her pen like a baton. She would maintain eye contact while nudging the Kleenex box across the table when Connie became emotional, a gesture that passed for sympathy and kept the ball rolling. The subject of sex came up during our second session, turning the spotlight on me. I sputtered as I tried to articulate my aversion to intimacy, pointing out ways in which "fooling around" had negative consequences from my experience, particularly in college.

"What do you mean by that?" came the question, and soon I was spilling my guts about attending a Collegiate party and meeting a co-worker's friend named Kim, whose ice-blue eyes and playful demeanor drew me to her. She wore a wide-brimmed hat without pretension, placing it on my head in the kitchen before standing back with crossed arms in mock appraisal, saying, "So what do we think?" Our flirtation continued during staff soirees at the bar across the street from the newsroom and finally at a house party that signaled the end of the spring semester, the sort of night where every song has hidden meanings and big-world burdens recede. The place was cramped with sweaty bodies, so we decided to take a walk and started making out in the empty back lot as light rain fell. Before long we were in primal mode on the wet grass, my knees muddied as I sought traction and she pulled her jeans down and off, eyes locked as our bodies thrashed. We returned to the house, caked with mud, laughing at our escapades and locking ourselves in the bathroom, where we showered as cursing partygoers pounded on the door. "Who is it?" Kim would coo in a sing-song voice, sparking renewed bursts of profanity.

Summer sent us in separate directions, and I was walking out of the communications building that fall when her friend approached me and suggested I give Kim a call, handing me a phone number. "Is there a reason you're involved in this?" I said, and she wheeled around and said, "Because she's pregnant, asshole." When I reached her, Kim told me that she was back home in Kalamazoo and would probably transfer to Western Michigan or the nearest community college. "This isn't going to happen between us, is it?" she asked, and I wasn't sure of her meaning. I said, "If you're asking if we're going to get married or something, my answer is that we barely know each other." I offered to help with the child if she chose to keep it, but she said she was going to have an abortion and that her mother had made the appointment. She needed nothing from me, a statement not as liberating as it might have sounded. I told her that I was grateful she had a support system and told her to call me if she was ever back in East Lansing. We never spoke again.

The fact that our backyard encounter had affected numerous lives might have raised a subconscious boundary for me, I explained to Stephanie and Connie. Perhaps I viewed sex as something wanton and potentially damaging, which made it difficult to engage in normal relations, even within the bond of marriage. Stephanie was patient with my theory but noted that contraception could make sexual intercourse a lot less "dangerous," if that was truly my concern. "I think it's a bunch of bullshit," said Connie, raising her palm to preemptively ward off the counselor. "I've heard that college story and I'm not diminishing it, but you shouldn't use it as a way to fashion some bizarre phobia that doesn't exist." Stephanie set down her pen, saying something about sexual hang-ups being quite real but at the same time understanding a spouse's frustration. "I think we need to change the dynamic a bit," she added, asking Connie to leave the room for a few moments so she could speak with me in private. I soon discovered the reason for this: She wanted to know if I was having an affair. "I just want to make sure I'm not missing an obvious reason for all this," she said, "one that you wouldn't be able to reveal in front of your wife. Sorry to be so direct, but that's sort of my job." I told her that not only was I not having an affair, I had been faithful to my wife since our wedding day, if we were talking about intercourse with other people. She looked at me to assess my candor and then said, "I heard a quote once that a man is only as faithful as his options – would that describe your situation?"

I responded that I liked to think my devotion went deeper than that. I told her about a young woman named Roberta who worked in advertising at the Gazette a decade earlier who flirted with me and accepted my attentions in return. She had olive skin and long dark hair and held her own in baseball conversations with the sports staff, flaunting her Minnesota Twins fandom with arcane statistics. Her desk was not far from mine, and when Connie visited the newsroom one day she asked, "Why is that girl looking over here?" I dismissed her concerns as foolish, which I thought them to be. Roberta knew I was married and surely had other romantic avenues. Flirting wasn't always a means to an end. But things came to a head the night before Thanksgiving, about a month after Connie spotted her in the newsroom. It was a raucous night at the Lantern and Roberta showed up with friends, preening in a tight tank top, sipping her drink from a straw. "Where's your wife?" she asked, and I told her she was at home. We went to the parking lot to avoid prying eyes and started kissing against the building, shielded by a bin where patrons pitched empty bottles. I pressed her hand down into my crotch, proud of my excitement, and she in turn took my hand and started leading me away. I didn't know where we were headed, but I remember stopping in my tracks, literally digging my heels into the pavement and saying I couldn't leave with her. She paused for a moment to see if I was serious and then said "suit yourself" before walking back into the bar with a jaunty stride, not bothering to look back.

The next day my family ate turkey and watched football, Connie's mother and aunt alongside us, Nathan wearing his Lions jersey and complaining when I lost track of the wishbone. We went around the table to express what we were thankful for, and when I choked up briefly talking about my blessings, they all thought it was touching rather than guilt breaking the surface. By the time I related this to our marriage counselor years later, things hadn't really changed, nor had they since. Connie and I enjoyed each other's company and were contented most days, but our respective relationships with our teenage son eclipsed the connection between husband and wife. "You're an incredible father," Connie once told me, "and a terrible husband." There was no use arguing. I thought back to a "Covid Chronicles" feature we did on a Sioux Falls woman who was one of the first confirmed cases in the state, and how her husband reacted to the diagnosis. They had rushed to the emergency room because the woman had sharp pains in her back and was having trouble breathing, and it turned out to be Covid-19 pneumonia, with abnormalities in her lungs. They were sent directly home and he cared for her, telling our reporter that "social distancing for us is the three dogs that sleep between us." The husband eventually contracted the virus but they gutted it out together, with help from neighbors and their married daughter, who happened to be a nurse. Going back to the hospital in the age of coronavirus meant possibly never seeing your loved ones again, so they spent their days at home, watching old movies, sharing their anguish, waiting for the world to heal. "The whole time I was hoping like hell that nothing happened to her," said the husband, "because I can barely take care of myself."

What was it like to lean on someone like that, allowing them to need you in return? Here I was hiding my symptoms, secretly plotting, when all Connie would have wanted was to help me, to the extent that she could, with unfiltered love. Hers was a kindness I didn't possess – a heart that when it sensed sadness from our Goldendoodle, Lillie, compelled Connie to roll on the carpet, all hugs and kisses, cajoling her back to joy. She saw kids at church without coats and made parkas appear, with no explanation, the following Sunday. Nathan told me about the time he stopped at a gas station with his mother and they saw a group of Native American teens who had run out of gas down the road and were wondering aloud about their next move. Connie went inside to get them a gas can and offered to drive them back to their car, which she did as Nathan marveled at the effortlessness of her actions. There were traits he admired in me, no doubt, but that gift of selflessness, or the effort one makes to foster it, was not one of them.

As my Covid symptoms steadied and I laid in bed, chills becoming less convulsive, revelations racked my soul. That was the true suffering. I thought about our marriage counseling, my antics at the strip club, my code of silence with Nathan. Notwithstanding whether I was a devoted husband or loving father, was I a good person? Did I make the world better? What were my contributions, exactly, beyond leading a newspaper and penning a pointed column here and there? Those were the doubts that came in the dark. I never once felt suicidal or lost hope. It was more like emotional inventory, an assessment of past failings, clinging to a belief that the mysteries of the next moment were worth seeking, no matter how foreboding.

I rolled over and smashed my pillow, desperate for sleep. My mind drifted back to the final session of our marriage counseling, when Stephanie had us turn to face each other and reveal something we had not shared before. Connie said that she still believed in me as a husband and that she appreciated me showing up for the appointments, which she knew had been difficult. She had experienced temptation through the years, a glass of wine on business trips that could have led to more, but she kept coming back to the conviction that our marriage was built on trust and worth fighting for, and she persevered. "That's the compact of love," she said. As they awaited my sentiments, Stephanie twirling her pen and Connie locking her gaze, I struggled to come up with something and panicked slightly before words and feelings started surging forward, as if finally unshackled. "I want to thank you for what you did that night in Washington D.C.," I told Connie. "You gave us a child. I was too stupid or selfish or flawed to do it, and you came to my side of things and persuaded me to be normal, just that one time, to make love to my wife and make a baby, and I don't want to think about what would have happened if I had rolled over or told you to get lost or done something horrible like that, I just don't want to think about it." Tears were streaming down my face, startling her to the point where she got up and wrapped her arms around me, embracing the life we had built together by fumbling in the darkness, trying to avoid obstacles in our way.

THIRTEEN

I spent most of the game against Yankton on the outer edges of Edison's football complex, shrouded in mask and stocking cap. I lied to Connie that I was too nervous to sit in the stands. The pumped-up student sections and late autumn chill created a pre-pandemic aura of playoff football, even with attendance limits in place. I thought about how many of these games I had covered as a sportswriter, working the press box or sideline as South Dakota's notoriously erratic weather took hold. Freezing rain turned one field into a gleaming ice sheet, players slipping and sliding to a dissatisfying 7-0 outcome. Then there was the team that attempted to punt into gale-force winds, watching in horror as the ball sailed backward over their heads and through their own end zone for a game-deciding safety. "Never seen a football do that," the grief-stricken coach told me in the locker room, players crouched and sniffling nearby. "Never want to see it again." I double-checked the forecast to make sure the elements, brisk with hardly a bluster, would spare Edison's postseason opener, a quarterfinal game the Nighthawks were favored to win. If they could get through their next two contests, the state championship would be played at the University of South Dakota's domed stadium, on statewide TV, with Nathan in a position to run crisp routes on artificial turf, breaking away from defenders. There was raw speed and football speed, I told him on numerous occasions, and he had the latter. He just needed Brad Hawkins to get him the ball. As I walked along the fence, avoiding eye contact with spectators, there was a rush of excitement from the stands. "Ladies and gentlemen, this is Nighthawk Country!" crooned the P.A. announcer as Edison's players ran onto the field in their scarlet and gray, Hawkins and Tommy Burgess leading the charge. The cheerleaders draped a handmade banner across midfield that the players tore through with gusto, leaving scraps of paper that represented the tattered remains of Yankton's title hopes. The game was a blowout, as Rick Schumacher had predicted. With his son setting the tone, Edison's offensive line created gaping holes to run through, helping the hosts build a 34-0 lead by halftime. Nathan made a few catches early in the game to set up touchdowns by Brad and Tommy, but Coach Talley summoned the reserves in the second half, an extended celebration for the Nighthawks as they looked ahead to the semifinals. I watched Nathan joke around with his teammates on the sideline, cheering for guys who rarely played and exhorting the students, who chanted "We can't hear you!" to Yankton fans who hadn't already crept to the parking lot. When the game was over and the scoreboard read 42-7, some of the Edison players tried to lift Talley on their shoulders before he angrily waved them off, pointing to the locker room. There was still work to be done, I could picture him saying. Save your celebration for the dome.

The election was three days later, forcing me out of my fog to help Gina and Cummings coordinate coverage. Most years, we would make sure pizza was ordered and set up newsroom command centers, juggling reporters and photographers while tracking results, plotting print layout and posting stories on the fly. Now we were doing all that remotely, minus the pizza. I told everyone they could put a slice or whole pie on their expense report, but it wasn't about the food. Trying to replicate the energy of an election-night newsroom in 2020 was sort of like cruising an online concert – you missed the collective buzz. "We're still chronicling history," Gina noted optimistically in our morning Zoom, trying to keep everyone on point. "For those of you who are out there doing the reporting, nothing much has changed." A few hours later, we broke a story about a seedy political activist arrested after police found hundreds of stolen campaign signs stowed in his garage, an effort to stem the tide of Republican domination, as he stated, "by any means necessary."

As we processed precinct reports that evening, it turned out that his sense of desperation was well-placed, and his sign-stealing gambit unsuccessful. South Dakota's red railing of one-party rule in the state legislature was not only reasserted but fortified in district races, leaving Democrats with just 11 members in the state House and

three in the Senate, the fewest in 66 years. Even the marijuana ballot measures, approved by voters to the surprise
of some pundits, faced an uphill battle, considering that
past initiatives of progressive persuasion were methodically
rebuffed by the legislature or right-leaning judges. "Same
shit, different year," a Democratic operative texted me as
attention turned to the presidential race, where his party's
hopes were considerably brighter, though still in doubt.
Lawton had pushed hard for Trump in battleground states
right up until the election, enriching her own campaign
coffers in the process. Given the possibility that a Trump
loss could spur him to run again in 2024, likely closing a
presidential window for the governor, she figured keeping
him in the White House was good for her political prospects,
not to mention her party.

When the networks called Florida for Trump as he
also led in other key states, it looked like he might beat the
odds and stay in office, causing one Gazette staffer to send
a photo of a mushroom cloud over the Slack channel before
deleting it. Cummings kept sending updates on betting odds
that showed Trump in good position, but the pendulum
swung when Fox News called Arizona for Biden and mail-in
ballots were counted in the wee hours in Pennsylvania,
Georgia, Michigan and Wisconsin, sparking unfounded cries
of chicanery from Trump and his supporters. By the next
morning, it was clear to anyone paying attention that Biden
would be the next president, but Lawton held the line. In
a conference call with reporters, she talked about how the
mainstream media and political establishment had stacked
the deck against Trump, dropping a reference to "rigged
election systems" that parroted the president's rhetoric and

raised eyebrows nationally, not to mention from the mayor of Sioux Falls.

Harper's office announced that he would hold a news conference the next day on the steps of City Hall, an unconventional move for an officeholder who wasn't on the 2020 ballot and had seen his party trounced across the state. The press release referenced support for stronger Covid restrictions, which led some to wonder why the mayor was staging an in-person media gathering, even if it was outdoors with masks required. We sent Patrick out with a photographer, and I couldn't resist heading downtown to lurk again in the shadows, a peripheral character in an increasingly confounding play. From a block away I could see signs of trouble. A group of F.A.R. members had staked out turf on the sidewalk, carrying signs that read "STOP THE STEAL!" and "MAYOR MUSSOLINI" while sniping at reporters and city personnel. I spotted Ed handing out leaflets and barking orders, offsetting his diminutive stature with the bearing of someone who longs to loom large. He had pulled a mask to his chin as a statement, its strings tangled with his ponytail in back. The weather was warm for early November, allowing Harper to approach the podium in Oxford shirt with rolled-up sleeves, forcing himself to look straight ahead and not at the protesters, who had managed to sniff out a press event that was not posted publicly. I could see him second-guessing himself and his staff for prizing the visual appeal of the City Hall steps over a more secure location inside the building, even with

Covid-related contingencies.

His shoulders slumped slightly before he steeled himself and began speaking loudly through a black-and-white mask bedecked with a simple message: DEMOCRACY. He began by referencing the national election and how it appeared Democrats would retake the White House, though "there are dangerous voices afoot that would have you believe that America is not a shrine to democracy, that our elections are suspect, tampered with, like some banana republic that requires outside influences to monitor systems, ensuring that there is no thumb on the scale." Rhetorical flourishes from debate, combined with the self-seriousness of student government and magnitude of leading a mid-sized American city, managed to keep his listeners in thrall. He was sharpening his knives for the governor.

"When I cast the tiebreaking vote to put forth a mask mandate in Sioux Falls, I noted that the policy was made necessary by a lack of adequate leadership in state government – more specifically, the governor's office," Harper said. "Today I find it disheartening that I must revisit the topic of leadership in the wake of the presidential election, because Governor Lawton has chosen to cast doubt on the outcome and jeopardize the peaceful transfer of power that makes our democracy the envy of the world – or used to." The F.A.R. members jeered from their spot on the sidewalk, shouting about voter fraud and dead people casting ballots, a Facebook feed come to life. Harper looked across the street as a police cruiser pulled up, no doubt called by one of his staffers, who were frantically working their phones while keeping an eye on Ed and his crew. The mayor pressed on. "It's sad that we're falling into the trap of those who wish to divide us, selling their lies in the pursuit of power, when we have so much work yet to do to help everyday citizens who are hurting from the ongoing pandemic. Again I find myself attempting to fill the void here in Sioux Falls, where I'll propose new measures to shut down indoor and outdoor dining, close bars, hair salons and other personal care services and limit retail stores to 20 percent capacity. I'm still looking at schools, but let it be known that personal responsibility is not enough. Telling people to wash their hands is not leadership. South Dakota ranks second among all states in per capita Covid cases and is on pace to have 100 deaths in just the first week of November. If Governor Lawton isn't going to step up and do something about it, then I will bear the burden myself."

Ed grew increasingly agitated as Harper laid out mitigation measures, swearing loudly and tossing his sign to the ground. He reached for something that turned out to be a bullhorn, which screeched with feedback as he struggled for the right volume and faced it at his foe. "Trump is still president because he doesn't treat us like sheep!" came Ed's amplified voice, a nasal intonation that nevertheless enlivened the zealots, whose roars led several police officers to cross the street. More squad cars had arrived since the mayor started speaking. Harper mentioned something about a private press event being hijacked, which led to a fresh bullhorn blast about the right to peacefully assemble. "Do you still believe in the First Amendment, you dime-store tyrant?" shouted Ed, who was cut off by the commotion of his son Eddie on the grass berm above the sidewalk, moving toward the mayor and waving around what later turned out to be a pocket Constitution. Harper backed toward the building as officers swarmed Eddie, clutching at his scrawny frame and

taking him to the ground as he continued to shout at the
mayor. I saw his glasses fly off as police worked to restrain
him, his efforts to retrieve them interpreted as an attempt
to flee. "Police brutality!" shouted Ed before a fresh phalanx
of officers arrived to seize his bullhorn and demand that the
group disperse, pointing out their lack of a permit. Eddie
was placed in a cruiser for the short trip to the police station,
and Ed got permission to retrieve his son's glasses, twisted
from the commotion. He made an attempt to straighten them
before placing them in his pocket, pausing on the berm to
stare toward City Hall's corner office before officers told him
to move on.

———————

Patrick's story highlighted Harper's proposed restrictions and
comments about the governor, noting the mayor's willingness
to stoke the flames of a searing political feud. We decided not
to lead with Eddie's incident, since he was released without being charged. There was no way to prove he meant
physical harm, according to authorities. "So why did they
throw him to the ground and restrain him?" asked Gina.
"Let me guess...they saw a public official in possible danger
and erred on the side of caution." Patrick said that wasn't
far off. According to his source, the officers thought Eddie
might have had a weapon that turned out to be the pocket
Constitution, a metaphor seemingly made for 2020. When a
well-heeled lawyer showed up demanding answers, police let
Eddie go but said they might reach out with further questions.
"We can mention the F.A.R. group and their outbursts after

dealing with Harper and Lawton," said Gina. "It's not like we're going to bury that incredible photo we got." The image showed Harper backing up the steps in a defensive posture while Eddie is wrestled to the ground by three uniformed cops, strands of hair covering his face as he stretches out his arms in a pleading gesture. I said we needed to make it clear in the cutline that he was reaching for his glasses rather than summoning some form of higher spirit. I wasn't keen on turning him into a martyr. "Either way," said Patrick, "it's probably the most interesting press conference photo I've ever seen."

Soon after the story posted I saw a call from Norah Newcombe's number on my phone and foolishly answered it, thinking we might get reaction from the governor's office. Instead she came out swinging once again, putting me on the defensive. "This is off the record, but you better start reining in your boy in the mayor's office," she said, immediately pissing me off by linking me to Harper's political decisions. "If he thinks it's time to get brave again just because the Democrats took advantage of Covid to get more absentee ballots to take down Trump, he's seriously mistaken." When I asked her if that meant she was admitting that Trump lost, there was silence. "The reason he lost," I told her, "is because he dropped the ball on pandemic response, so it seems to me that Harper holding a press conference to talk about a more responsible approach isn't a terrible idea."

I could hear her breathing in short bursts through the phone, which I took as an anger management exercise. "Your political naivete is showing," she told me. "You think grandstanding on the steps of City Hall and attacking the governor is going to win people over, or will it just make

him look like a charlatan? Maybe you didn't see the election
results from across the state. Do you think South Dakota is
thirsting for a liberal Democrat mayor to tell them how to
run their lives and businesses?" They might be in Sioux Falls,
I told her. Biden got 44 percent of the vote here, as opposed
to 35 percent statewide. But who was I to lecture someone
who had been involved in South Dakota politics for almost
a whole year? I could hear her exhaling into the void before
getting back on the phone, and for the first time I legiti-
mately worried about her mental health. "Listen, asshole,"
she sneered. "Do you think the F.A.R. guys are going to take
much more of this shit? Mask mandates? Restaurants shut
down? Maybe even schools? I know these guys, I know what
they stand for, and they're not going to let the suffocating
government overreach that screwed up other places happen
here. You're not in fucking Michigan anymore. They've tried
to explain to you what's at stake here and reach out to you in
various ways. Why do you think your son's on that football
team? It would be wise to use your authority as editor of the
state's largest newspaper to restore some sanity to City Hall
before these guys decide to knock your dick in the dirt. Are
we clear? Terrific. Goodbye."

FOURTEEN

Walking into the Gazette had a calming effect, even on days I dreaded the work. The yellow-brick building represented stability and purpose, set apart from offices where mundane tasks were performed. At its best, a newspaper serves as community compass, serving notice when things veer off track but otherwise charting the journey with a sense of direction, delivered without fail. A few months after arriving in Sioux Falls, I was asked to give the sports rundown at the Gazette's daily news meeting, which took place in a wood-paneled conference room with all the top editors, a formidable gathering in those days. An afternoon deluge had snarled traffic, judging by the chorus of car horns from the street below. As editors went around the room with planned coverage, discussing next steps and front-page priorities, a swell of emotion hit me, unexpected but recognizable once it arrived. It was homesickness stirred with the realization that my future was laid out for me, in a place I hadn't previously known existed, raising the prospect that the random series of events that led me to Sioux Falls weren't random at all, but a confluence of the episodes of my young life. There was a catch in my throat when it was my turn to speak, causing concerned looks, but I powered through it, savoring the feeling of being part of the process. I loved the care with which each newspaper was curated, as ephemeral as it was, destined for the trash heap except on rare occasions when it was set aside for posterity, brittle like parchment in a scrapbook or attic. Even with the advent of the internet, for which the industry was ill-prepared, there was enough financial heft from print revenue that the compass remained viable, but the reef was always waiting. The crunch of the Covid crisis accelerated our demise as community vanguard, and now meetings were a few people huddled in front of computer screens, flailing at the reality of more news to cover with fewer reporters and cratering revenue. Not long after my disturbing phone call from Newcombe, I got an email from corporate outlining voluntary buyout opportunities for employees with certain lengths of service, including myself. The new CEO, fresh off running a hedge fund, wanted to appease shareholders by cutting expenses and paying down debt. He also wanted to unload real estate, which meant the Gazette building, an empty husk of the journalistic hub that gave meaning to my life and so many others, was on the market, a compass only capable of projecting its descent.

I drove down to the Gazette the night after the City Hall debacle, confident no one would be there. There was a moment of suspense when I wondered if my keycard would work. The place smelled the same, a nostalgic blend of newsprint and recycled air, and the only light on the second floor came from mounted monitors displaying online trends – clicks for each article, engagement time, heaviest traffic periods.

These analytics steered us toward stories we knew people would read, a valuable tool but enlightening to a fault, like when a man caught masturbating at the library outperformed a series on school-age kids living in poverty. We told ourselves that good journalism resonates regardless of clicks, but advertisers didn't always agree. "Severed head in road – click for details," came a voice from the newsroom, startling me. I looked over to see the silhouette of Cummings, reclining at his desk and staring at the screens. "We used to joke that the county could raise property taxes ten-fold," he said, "but if the home page had a story about a severed head in the road, that would get more clicks – although the art might have been a problem." I decided to play along. "Depends on whether the head was smiling or not," I said, and his laugh was more of a sigh. After years of seeing him exhibit various moods, from angry to energetic to outraged, this was the first time I had ever heard him sound defeated. I was about to ask him why he was sitting alone in the dark, but he beat me to it. "I needed to be here to find an anchor, or maybe a lifeline," he said. "When things were swirling out of control, it was always nice to walk into this building and embrace the work. We were doing important shit, and that balanced out the bad stuff. I know that you felt that way, too. Maybe that's why you're here."

I pulled up a chair as he kept talking. "Let me tell you something I don't think I've ever told you – you're an incredible writer," he said. "I would have killed to have that gift, to make words flow like that and hear their rhythm in your mind. It was always like work to me, like laying bricks, and the sentences never set on each other as smoothly as they should have. So I found other ways to make myself useful

– you know what I'm talking about – the guy to call when someone's screen froze up or we couldn't find something in the archive, the guy that never gets his face in the paper but still busts his ass to get breaking news posted, with someone else's byline. That didn't mean I had to like it. I had a lot of reasons to resent you even before that night when I went banging on your door, knowing my wife was inside. That just gave me a better excuse." He was leaning forward and hanging his head, elbows on knees. A computer buzzed nearby. "When I confronted Pam that night, she told me you guys didn't have sex, but I knew it wasn't from lack of effort on her part. I figured I had to live with her, though, so you were the one I blamed. I wanted to still be married to her. I was scared not to be. The problem was that she knew that and resented me for it, saw it as weak, and tested it over and over, until she found someone she wanted for good and never came back." I asked him when that happened and he said about a year ago, which meant all those Zoom jokes about household chores were not marital responsibilities, as Gina and I assumed, but an effort to create the illusion of domestic normalcy. Cummings had quarantined alone.

"Don't feel too sorry for me," he said. "This is sort of hard to say, and please keep it between us, but I wasn't by myself all the time. I became a little bit friendly with Norah Newcombe." I thought he was joking for a second, but he kept staring down at the carpet.

"Norah Newcombe from the governor's office?" I said. "You can't be serious. The one who just reamed my ass yesterday and has been threatening me about the Lawton-Harper feud? The far-right psycho who has questioned our journalistic integrity from the beginning? That Norah Newcombe?"

"That's the one," said Cummings. "I'm not proud of it, believe me. She was in Sioux Falls one night and wanted to introduce herself in person to improve the working relationship between Lawton's office and the Gazette. She said she had done the same thing with you."

"That's bullshit," I said, racking my brain to remember any entreaties on her part. "If she ever reached out like that, I would have turned her down."

"Apparently you're more noble than I am – or more married," he said. "I mean, you have to admit she's not hard to look at. We had drinks at that dive bar on Western, she asked me a ton of questions, I asked some of her, and we went back to her hotel room. It was basically a one-night thing. A man has needs, after all."

I still expected him to jump up and reveal his prank, flicking on the lights as staffers emerged from behind desks, howling at my discomfort. But he just sat there like a piece of shit, waiting for my reaction. "Do you have any idea how unethical it is for you to have a sexual relationship with Lawton's main communications and policy person when we're trying to provide objective coverage of the governor during a public health crisis? Were either of you worried about Covid, or did your romantic yearnings sort of take over?"

"I could ask the same thing about a certain strip joint near Mitchell," he responded.

My heart rate accelerated before he even completed the sentence. I stood up and asked him what the hell he was talking about. "Let's just say Norah has a working knowledge of what the F.A.R. boys are up to," he told me. "Some of them were in Michigan when she spoke to militia groups about their rights and how to plan protests – a constitutional boot

camp, if you will, for the conservative cause. She made good
money on it before coming here, and I wouldn't mess with
her if I were you. The ideology is strong with that one."

A few things were starting to make sense, such as
Lawton knowing about Harper's threat to close schools and
F.A.R. showing up at the City Hall press conference. And
Cummings' willingness to help with my hunting trip no
longer seemed like a friendly gesture. My head ached with the
realization that Newcombe, in addition to pestering me for
information, had groomed a mole in the managerial structure
at the Gazette, and Cummings had let it happen. "I'm taking
the buyout," he informed me as I was deciding whether to
fire him on the spot. "I think it would be easier for both of
us if you just let me do that rather than bringing up all this
stuff to corporate. That would be a pretty messy road for
everybody involved."

As I tossed aside my chair and started walking toward
the stairs, he called out to me: "Hey, we had a pretty good
run, didn't we?"

"Fuck you," I said.

———

The state activities association announced the next morning
that Edison's semifinal game would not be played. Rapid City
had ended its season because of a surge of positive cases and
close contacts within the high school, forcing the district to
return to distance learning. "I saw a text about that...what
does it mean?" asked Nathan when I told him. His sense of
taste had returned, and he was eating peanut butter toast

while watching videos on his phone. The fact that he looked up meant that he cared about my answer. "Well, it means Edison just advanced to the championship game," I said. "Rapid City had to forfeit, so you guys are in. I would rather have done it the old-fashioned way, but welcome to 2020, I guess." The other semifinal was Catholic Central against Watertown, and it would take a miracle for Watertown to win, so all signs pointed to Sioux Falls rivals Edison and Central in the title game, on artificial turf and under the lights, a dream come true. "What if the state finals are called off?" said Nate, starting to pack up his stuff for school. "How would they know who's state champion?" I shrugged him off like there was no possibility of that happening. "You just worry about how you're going to beat Central," I told him. "That's gonna be a hell of a game, and it will happen. Just trust me on that."

After he left I started writing, surprised at how easily the sentences flowed. I wrote about remote learning, what a disaster it had been the previous spring, and how studies showed vast swaths of students falling off the educational grid when not in physical classrooms. I noted how only a tiny fraction of school-age kids nationally had been hospitalized due to coronavirus when compared with the general population, meaning students who contracted the virus would recover without taking up hospital beds. As for teachers, there had certainly been positive cases since school opened in the fall, but not the torrent that activists and union leaders predicted, and most students complied with the expectation that they wear masks. I wrote about a conversation I had with the school board president, whose son also attended Edison. She agreed with me that classes needed to remain in session and that Harper would be making a mistake if he stepped in. "This has been a success story so far," she said. "Nobody thought it would be perfect and that there would be no infections, but we have managed to open our doors every day and provide as close to a normal learning environment as we can, and that has a lot of value."

When I asked her if the mayor had the authority to shut down in-person schooling, she said that the board's attorney would not fight it, citing emergency powers written into the city's charter. "It's Harper's ballgame," she told me off the record. "I don't even think the city council could stop him on this one." By the time my fingers stopped moving I had written a thousand words, capping it off with this conclusion: "Here's one thing we know for sure: There is more to school than the giving and returning of assignments. An impressionable mind in the hands of a skilled teacher can shine a light that lasts a lifetime. We believe the mayor understands this and will do the right thing, regardless of political motivations, and we thank him for his wisdom in these matters." I didn't even ask anyone to give it a read. I put a headline on it and posted it myself under the banner of a Gazette editorial, flexing my executive muscles. It received a flurry of attention online, with parents of school-age kids offering support. Those who saw rising Covid numbers as a major threat and schools as a reflection of community concerns were livid, accusing the editorial board of turning its back on the pressure campaign for greater mitigation. Several announced on social media that they would cancel their digital subscriptions, which I assumed were activated at the discount rate.

The reaction from Gina was more troubling, even though I knew the call was coming. She asked me if I had posted the editorial by mistake before she and Cummings could read it, and I told her no. I had decided to use my unilateral authority on an issue with which I had unique insight, and time was of the essence. I didn't want the message to get bogged down in our usual back and forth. "By back and forth, do you mean the deliberative process we use to determine the board's stance on important topics?" she said. "The process we've used for every Gazette editorial since I've been around and the one used by just about every newspaper in the world? Is that the one you decided to blow off for some reason that I won't speculate on because of my remaining respect for you?" Those words struck a nerve, so I offered a condescending reply about the trend of newspapers dismantling editorial boards due to shrinking staffs and ambiguous barriers between opinion and news coverage. "We have three people on a board that used to be much larger," I said, "and we're going to be down to two with Cummings leaving, which means we don't really have a board."

Silence on the other end suggested that she hadn't heard the news, so I told her that Cummings was taking a buyout and his Gazette days were over. I considered the stuff with Newcombe to be a personnel issue and didn't bring it up, although she probably deserved to know. "When were you going to tell me that?" she said. "That's going to require a lot of reshuffling to get stuff edited and posted, not to mention just the common courtesy of keeping me informed on a major shakeup. I have to say that you've been a little absent over the past week, and now I see that we're taking random editorial stances without my knowledge, thanking the mayor for 'his wisdom in these matters,' as if this was North Korea and he was our Dear Leader. I mean, how worried should I be right now, on a scale of 1 to 10?" I tried to talk her down, saying we would move a reporter into an editing role to fill the void temporarily while exploring the possibility of making a hire. Cummings was important but not irreplaceable and we would find a way forward, like we always did. "I'll take that as a seven," she said, tossing me a hint of humor like a scrap. "We've had challenges before, but this just feels different," she added. "I wake up every day wanting to think our work matters, but lately it's just been people taking sides of the Covid issues and following that trail wherever it goes, whether it makes sense as journalism or not. That's not the newspaper I know, and it's not what I signed up for, but I need the paycheck so I'll keep grinding, for now at least. Our readers deserve that much."

She hung up rather than await my response, and I wavered on my way up the basement stairs. All the progress my immune system had made against the disease seemed jeopardized by distress. Cummings had conspired against me and Gina was losing faith, and there was no way to just call everyone into a meeting room to talk it over and fix it. The damage I had done, the damage being done to me, was likely irreversible. There was an odd comfort in that, after years of dealing with penny-ante obstacles and arguments at work, play-acting at resolving conflicts that amounted to nothing. Facing an existential threat made me feel something, a professional form of self-harm. "Everything all right?" Connie asked as I passed the kitchen, and I lied that I just needed some air. "Take the dog with you!" she called, and Lillie came tumbling down the steps to the backyard, sniffing and digging as I walked along, scanning houses across the way. I wondered whether those people shared my anxiety or enjoyed non-dramatic contented lives, pressed together by the pandemic and mirthful without trying. Was it possible? My life seemed stretched rather than compressed, each tangent filled with tests and trials that exposed my vulnerabilities. Even the dog seemed hard to read. Inside she was fluffy and frivolous, playing with stuffed toys and rolling around with Nathan and Connie, enjoying their company. When I took her out back, as I did more often since Covid, she reverted to primal instincts, leaving skeletal tokens of conquests, freed from domestic constraints. This is who I am, she announced with each mouse or bird carcass. And who was I? My mind trembled at the thought, summoning images of my own animal instincts and where the limits of their influence might lie.

FIFTEEN

The speeches seemed to go on forever. First the principal and then the athletic director stood in front of half-filled bleachers in the Edison gym, using words like "courage" and "resilience" to praise coaches and athletes during a "challenging season for all of us." The players were spaced out in folding chairs on the court, fidgeting in jerseys and masks, while cheerleaders stood to the side, puzzled at the scarcity of spirit-worthy moments. "Is this supposed to be a pep rally?" Connie whispered in my ear. "I think they forgot the pep." Parents were summoned to the Wednesday afternoon function, two days before the state championship game, to honor the football team and get ticket information for the showdown against Catholic Central, which had routed Watertown. But with the general student population kept away to reduce crowding, it felt like another meeting that could have been handled by email. Nathan confirmed as much by leaning his head back with arms crossed, mask askew and eyes half closed.

The athletic director, a former basketball coach whose

ascension to a higher salary bracket was contingent on adopting school district orthodoxy, approached the end of his remarks. "Keep in mind that we organized this gathering and allowed it to happen because the kids deserve it," he said. "In the event that something happens, and we make a switch to remote learning, this will also serve as the post-season banquet for a team that truly has been a credit to Nighthawk Nation. Regardless of whether the championship game is played, these boys have made us proud!" Several parents recoiled at that last statement, and Dale Burgess actually stood and thrust both arms at the AD as if to dismiss him entirely. Cap was nowhere to be seen, and I shuddered to think what his reaction would be to this administrative strategy of laying the groundwork for bad news. The school resource officer, whose job it was to provide a police presence at Edison, stood against the gym wall, surveying the stands. Coach Talley signaled to Dale and other parents to tone it down, but I could see he was agitated as well. The former college running back maintained an aura of athletic vigor despite an accumulation of weight since his playing days, and he showed some agility on his way to the podium.

"I probably shouldn't say this, but I can't believe what I'm hearing," he said after grabbing the microphone and yanking his mask down to his chin, allowing his mustache to breathe. "These young men behind you have a chance to do something this school hasn't accomplished in two decades – win a state football title – and all I hear is gloom and doom. I mean, it feels like a funeral in here." Several parents clapped in agreement and Dale shouted "Amen, brother!" The athletic director made a move toward the podium, but the principal pulled him back. "One thing we can agree on is that we're proud of these boys," Talley continued. "They followed all the rules, jumped through all the hoops, because they just wanted to play football and they got that chance. And when we asked them to do extraordinary things on the field, apart from all that other crap, they answered the bell, every single time. Brad Hawkins, Tommy Burgess, Cale Schumacher...I could go on and on, but these senior leaders refused to dwell on the negatives and tried to give this school something to get excited about again, and their job is not yet finished. I don't know about you, but we will be showing up at that dome on Friday night ready to fight for a state championship, because playing it safe is not an option." Most of the parents and players were on their feet at this point, urging him on. The cheerleaders responded by waving their pom-poms and kicking at the air, buoyed by the shift in mood. "Not showing up is not an option!" Talley shouted. "Not manning up is not an option! And not beating the hell out of Central in the biggest game of our lives – that is not an option!" Connie and I looked at each other and rose to our feet to join the chorus of hoots and howls, the volume of which was ear-splitting. The clearly relieved resource officer was on the court high-fiving players, oblivious to the principal avoiding the hoopla and sitting with his head in his hands, pondering the potency of a slow-simmering secret.

The call from Harper came later that night as I edited stories for morning release, part of an increased workload meant to ease tensions with Gina. Our Zoom calls and messages were cordial, fulfilling the bare minimum of interaction it required to put out the paper, but the editorial still hung in the air like a foul odor, especially after I muscled it into Sunday print. When no formal complaint arrived from the mayor's office, I attributed the silence to either Harper's busy schedule or an admission that my arguments were persuasive. As it turned out, he was building up steam for the phone call. "That was quite a manifesto," he began, indicating that small talk was a privilege to which I was no longer entitled. "I wasn't expecting a preemptive shot from a media organization I trusted with background information on this issue." I told him my arguments had nothing to do with our conversations, that I sincerely believed keeping schools open was the proper course. "Interesting," he said, with a sarcastic edge. "It must be nice to be able to have opinions with no real-life consequences, but some of us don't have that luxury. I don't know if you've seen the latest Covid data, but it's disturbing. Hospitalizations and deaths are rising, and schools can't be separated from the community at large. It's one big ecosystem, newspaper editors and football players included. So here's the deal, off the record for now, because I think I can still trust you: I'm going to announce Friday morning that Sioux Falls public school buildings are closing and we're going back to remote learning, starting Monday. That gives everyone a chance to bring their laptops home and get ready for the new phase. All activities will be discontinued starting Friday, which means Edison will not participate in the football game Friday night. I'm not sending our students and families into a domed environment under the current conditions, no matter how important the game is."

The words hit me like a prophecy finally unfurled. It

was almost a relief to know a decision had been made, as misguided as I thought it was, so the fallout could begin, after weeks of worrying and waiting. I told him that backlash from parents and students would be severe, and that it seemed cruel to allow teams to keep practicing before pulling the plug at the last minute. "We're still figuring out some elements of the plan, tying it in with other mitigation measures," said Harper. "It's not ready yet, in other words, and when it is, we'll move forward regardless of whom it offends. I didn't take this job to make decisions based on who would love me or hate me. I took it to make a positive difference in people's lives, and this is consistent with that approach. If you don't like it, well, I guess you'll just have to respect my wisdom in these matters."

I drove down to Cap's shop the next day to tackle the issue head-on, fearing what he would do if he heard the news from someone else. The place was slightly less cluttered than my last visit, and I was glad to find him alone, twisting a wrench into an overturned snowblower, body contorted on one knee, beer bottle nearby. He knew it was me without looking up. "How was the pep rally?" he asked. "I heard Coach Talley stole the show by telling those bastards to stick their protocols up their ass." I said that was an accurate summation, and it was good to see the boys fired up after their last game was called off, but there were other complications to consider. "What the fuck does that mean?" he said, looking up at me. "Either we play football or we don't. What's complicated about that?" Rather than dance around the subject, I told him of Harper's plans, but only after getting him to promise that he wouldn't spread it around. Things would be bad enough when the announcement came the next morning. As I laid out the scenario, he craned his neck downward, and for a moment I thought it was a sign of resignation that there was nothing we could do. That illusion was shattered by shrieks of metallic clatter as he flung his wrench across the room.

"You were supposed to take care of this, you mother-fucker!" he shouted while getting to his feet, face red with rage. "Why didn't you talk some sense into him? Are you such a shithead that your articles don't carry weight anymore?"

As unnerved as I was by his anger, I was pretty fed up myself. His habit of blaming me for other people's actions was getting old. "What does this have to do with me?" I said. "I can't wave a magic wand and make government policies disappear. I've been up front with you from the beginning while you've schemed behind my back. What's this bullshit about Norah Newcombe using F.A.R. connections to influence people at the Gazette – some undercover operation to keep the football season alive?"

"You're damn right it is!" said Cap. "And to keep Harper from ruining everything else with his liberal bullshit. Why do you think we wanted your son on the fuckin' team? If you think it's because of his pass-catching ability, you're dumber than I thought. We wanted you to tone down your BS about lockdowns and have a way to get to you, to stop your goddamned 'Covid Chronicles' from poisoning the well. We also figured you had a way to get to Harper, which is what we need right now."

I thought back to Newcombe's comment about Nathan

making the team and felt a wave of nausea. If it were true, he could never find out. Those summer texts from Brad had legitimized my son's athletic aspirations as well as mine, helping to rekindle our connection. The thought of them being merely a ploy in some convoluted plot was too much to fathom, and I pushed it out of my mind. I told Cap that there were ways to influence policy without all the cloak and dagger stuff. I offered to reach out to Harper again and plead our case, but he waved me off, saying he would do the pleading from now on. He was pacing the floor and asking rapid-fire questions about my meetings with Harper at Chatham Park – where exactly they took place, who arrived first, how long we stayed. He took in the information and thought for a while before walking up to where our chests were almost touching, and I could smell the beer on his breath.

"Listen to me closely, because this is what's going to happen," he said. "You're going to call Harper and arrange one of those meetings for tomorrow morning at 6 a.m. I've got him pegged for an early riser. The only difference is that we are going to be the ones who show up to talk about this school closing bullshit and why it doesn't make sense for the kids."

I wasn't quite sure what he was getting at. "Who's 'we' in that scenario?" I asked.

"Either Ed or myself. We'll keep Eddie away because he's probably being monitored after his theatrics the other day."

"Harper is not going to want to meet with you guys," I told him.

"What are you, fucking stupid? You're not going to tell him it's us. You're going to tell him that you have some fresh dirt on Lawton, something about emails showing her falsifying Covid data or some shit like that. Something to get his dick hard, and we'll be sitting there in a white Ford Escape when he shows up, ready to plead our case."

"Sitting in my car, you mean?"

"No one's going to take your car. Relax. I can line up an Escape from one of my body shop buddies. Might not be as pretty as yours, but it'll look fine at six in the morning."

"I'm not comfortable with this," I told him. "You're not going to be able to change Harper's mind, and what's he going to say to me after your little shakedown? He'll never trust me or the paper again. This is bad from every angle."

"Every angle, huh? OK, sure," Cap said. "What about the angle of a high school senior who works his ass off all summer for football season and goes undefeated to make the state championship game, reaching a goal he's had since he started strapping it on for pee wee football. What about the angle of a parent who's watched his son go through all that and has a chance to play for something he never attained, but it gets pulled away because of a political pissing match that isn't really about the virus?"

I stood my ground but stayed silent, racking my brain for another way to reach him. His face was ugly up close, scarred from a life of chasing after his failures, as if he could overtake them. He reached into his pocket for his phone.

"I've got another angle for you, pal," he told me. "How about this one from a family man who has his finger on the pulse of the community?" He fiddled with the phone and pointed it toward me so I could see an image I instantly recognized. It was a photo of me on a couch with my head tilted back and a strawberry blonde woman on her knees, going about her business. "I would hate for sweet Connie to have to see what you were up to that night," Cap said.

"You son of a bitch!" I shouted while grabbing at the phone, which he pulled away with a laugh.

"Don't pretend you didn't have a great fucking time on that hunting trip," he said. "I know you don't want to insult my intelligence by telling me that. You were finally alive, for a day at least, without the shit you surround yourself with to pretend you're not like me. Crapped on by your old man, guilty from things gone wrong, and now wanting to see your son have his time in the spotlight without some uppity mayor taking it away to further his career. You wouldn't have hidden your Covid symptoms and those of your son if you didn't feel the same way, am I right?"

I was backing toward the door, shaken by all that he knew about me, the position I had put myself in. My family, my reputation, my career, maybe my life, all in the hands of these people. The worst part was that I wanted the same thing they wanted and had sunk to their depths to get it.

"Don't forget to make that phone call," said Cap before turning back to his work. "I'll let you see yourself out."

———

Harper surprised me by answering the phone. I thought maybe he felt he had gotten the final word on the subject and that would be it, but there was still a level of familiarity and trust, precisely what Cap wanted to exploit. I heard myself saying the words I had rehearsed in my home office, away from Connie and Nathan, trimming traces of artifice from my voice. It had to sound convincing, and it was. A source had sent documents that appeared to show Governor Lawton and her staff altering coronavirus data and covering it up to make her response to the pandemic look better than it was. We weren't quite ready to run with the story, but it was political hemlock for her if we connected the dots.

Harper asked for more information and I said I couldn't discuss it over the phone. If he could meet me at the park the next morning, I would hand over copies and he could evaluate them himself. The excitement in his voice, and the fact that he texted me later to confirm the time, told me he would be there. For just a moment, I considered changing course and telling him about Cap and Ed and their plans. Maybe we could get the police involved to charge them with extortion, or at least scare them off, making them go underground. But those were thoughts that didn't lead to action. I knew them from experience. They emerged merely to make me feel better, as if my conscience was in there somewhere, bound and gagged, rather than not existing at all.

SIXTEEN

In my dream Nathan is in the Fourth of July parade but as a teenager, pedaling with legs akimbo on a child's bike, suffused with patriotic glow. He's tooting his horn and enjoying the pageantry as I follow along on the sidewalk, waving and calling his name. No matter how much commotion I make, he doesn't look my way. The sun sears the back of my neck. He picks up speed on the downward slope toward the park, legs churning cartoonishly as he races past dignitaries and colorful floats. I increase my own pace, weaving through spectators, screaming "Stop him!" to a cluster of firefighters parading abreast their truck. They take no notice as he sails past. My head throbs in the heat. A woman standing outside a shop says, "You should have taught him how to stop," and I see that it's Connie, arms folded, unwilling to help, wearing the sun dress from the first night we met. As my feet hit the grass of the park, cushioning my stride, I marvel at my speed, urging myself on before realizing I've lost track of Nathan. At the end of the parade route, bikes are neatly aligned. Kids hug their parents, chattering about

flag bearers and fire engines, red-faced from the ride. There's
no sign of Nathan. I stumble past them onto an empty street
approaching the intersection, exhausted and screaming for
help. A police officer is on his radio, watching warily. "What's
the matter with you people?" I scream, as someone grabs me
from behind. "Where the hell is my son?"

<hr />

I woke up Friday morning drenched in sweat and hounded
by cerebral fog, an unwelcome companion since my bout with
Covid. The prospect of starting the day with a clear head
seemed elusive. I'd read studies showing that mental fatigue
from coronavirus could last weeks or months or even years,
a result of the virus infiltrating brain tissue. Psychological
factors played a role, which put me at risk. I felt guilty about
putting Harper in position to be harangued, again, by Covid
truthers, under the guise of opposition research. As I lay
in bed recounting our conversation, I was sure he would
angrily rebuff the F.A.R. overtures, but perhaps I was wrong.
Morning came and went with no announcement from City
Hall or the school district about remote learning, and the
state championship game was still on. I spoke with Nathan
before he left for school, trying to animate my voice to match
the magnitude of the occasion.

He was wearing his football jersey, a school tradition
on game days, and had taken pains to get his hair looking
perfectly chaotic, making me self-conscious about my dishev-
elment. "Bus leaves at 2," he said when I asked him about
class dismissal. "We get to do a walkthrough on the field down

there to get used to the turf. Coach is having us bring two pairs of shoes to get the right tread." I told him about some of the games I had covered in the dome and how the air gets heavy on the field, making it harder to breathe. I told him to stay focused and hydrated and not waste energy on anything but the action. He nodded and said, "We talked about that on the group chat. No trash talking, just take care of business. The seniors mentioned this is the only shot they'll ever get – they don't want to blow it." I told him I was proud of him and the way he handled it all, being the new guy on the team and fighting through Covid and other complications. He looked at me and I wondered if he could sense my self-contempt, the lengths to which I had gone to make this game possible. If so, he didn't reveal it. As he stuffed a folder into his backpack and headed to the door, I asked to take a picture of him in his jersey. "Really?" he remarked. "I'm sort of late." Just give me a second, I said, and he played along, standing up straight and smiling dutifully, school about to begin.

———

I worked for a while and then snuck in a nap, trying to shake my fatigue. It would probably be a late night, win or lose. I was a bit surprised I hadn't heard from Harper, but maybe no news was good news. It didn't make sense to highlight my role in the arrangement by reaching out to him. Soon enough, though, I would need to explain myself, and I tried to imagine how that conversation would go. Should I tell him that I was forced into compliance by Cap and his crew, or would that lead to more problems? I tried to picture his face when he realized our rendezvous had taken a drastic turn and he would get a lecture on school closures rather than collecting evidence of Lawton's malfeasance. His anger had flared a few times recently, but nothing as justifiable as this. He would never trust me again, I told myself, a concern Cap had shrugged off as inconsequential, as if journalists could turn credibility on and off like a spigot. I had worked hard for the things I was throwing away, a foundation of building trust with sources, verifying data, correcting mistakes. People like Cap and Ed had never existed within such guardrails and had no estimation of their value. They saw people as opportunities or obstacles in relation to things they wished to achieve, with Harper and me part of the assembly line, or pieces to be dismantled.

It seemed odd to be balancing the weight of that threat with preparations for the biggest game of Nathan's life, the kind of atmosphere I had only dreamed of as a kid. I thought of my father and his pride in my hockey exploits, and how he would have handled a situation like this. Any other year, both of my parents might have made the trip to South Dakota to watch their grandson play, but the pandemic made that impossible, so I told them I would send updates. "Tell Nate to take off those damn gloves," my dad wrote in an email after I forwarded regular-season highlights. "Those actually make it more difficult to catch the ball, if you look at the studies." I was tempted to ask him if those were the same studies that showed wearing masks caused oxygen deficiency, but I thought better of it. There were enough of those arguments ongoing without starting a new one. My mom, as usual, took the opposite approach, asking me about Covid protocols and if playing the game was consistent with safety measures, and I assuaged her concerns without bringing up Harper's apprehension. When she followed up by asking if Nathan was having fun, I laughed at the question and chided her for asking it before realizing that I honestly didn't know the answer.

"Which one should I wear?" said Connie, gesturing at the vast array of Edison High spirit wear on her bed. She had faithfully combed the school website for merchandise before the season began, arming herself with T-shirts, pullovers and trucker hats to show support for her son, despite only a passing interest in football. I hadn't shared with her Cap's remark about Nathan making the team for deceitful reasons, and I never would. I had also kept her in the dark about setting up the F.A.R. meeting with Harper, which would have caused her to lose as much respect for me as I had lost for myself. Shame is a solo journey, and it seemed emblematic of our marriage that something that occupied so many of my thoughts was locked and distanced from my wife, an annex she didn't know existed. I gestured toward a Nighthawks sweatshirt and told her we needed to leave soon to claim our seats. It was about an hour drive to the college campus and the dome seated 8,000, or half that with Covid restrictions. I found my Edison long-sleeve and threw it on, feeling a little better as the day went on without flare-ups, meaning the game would go on and Harper wasn't trying to get me fired, at least not yet.

———

I talked briefly with Gina about sports coverage before Connie and I headed south on the interstate, trading the sprawling expanse of strip malls and subdivisions for soggy pastoral scenes. We talked about the difference between this football season and Nathan's pee wee experience, when he wore shoulder pads two sizes too large and endured countless calamities. "I shouldn't laugh," said Connie, recalling the game when Nate emerged from a pile of tangled bodies with helmet askew, as if his head rotated beneath the scrum. "Our hearts skipped a beat too many times that year," she told me, adding that he was probably too little to be seriously hurt. "Tell that to the kid who broke his collarbone," I said. We both knew that season had been an affront to my overly cautious parental leanings, and it seemed worlds away from where we found ourselves now, breaking down the matchup with Catholic Central, just one win from a state championship, my mental anguish softened by the rumble of the road. We were about halfway there when I felt a buzz from my phone and looked down to see a text from Cap. "Call me," it said. "We got a problem."

It was too risky to call with Connie in the car, so I had to let those words fester. The respite I enjoyed from otherwise relentless anxiety, a brief period in the car with my wife on the way to my son's football game, was over. I pondered possible scenarios, from Harper deciding to cancel the game to him reaching out to the police about being coerced, which could bring my involvement to light. It was deeply unsettling to run through scenarios that Cap considered a problem. "Are you OK?" asked Connie. I realized I was sweating profusely and gripping the wheel like a vise, trying to keep my hands from shaking. "Just nervous about the game," I said, unable to utter much more than that. A few minutes later I broke the silence by telling her I needed to make a phone call as soon as we parked, but she put up a fight, saying we needed to get inside to save our spots. I pictured Cap pacing and muttering while expecting my call. The concourse was already crowded as we made our way into the stadium and found two seats around the 40-yard line. Parents were standing to survey the sheen of the synthetic turf field, its end zones adorned with school names and colors. A few Catholic Central players were out for early warmups, tossing a football as coaches chatted nearby. "I can't believe our son is going to play on that field," said Connie, getting out her phone to take a few pictures. I took that as my cue to excuse myself, walking briskly back into the concourse to call Cap.

"What the hell's going on?" I said when he picked up.

He stammered for a few seconds, cursing himself before taking a breath and finally saying, "He's dead."

"What are you talking about? Who's dead?" I had to keep my voice down while moving along the corridor. After a while I found an unlocked door and ducked into a reception room, trying to sort out what Cap was telling me.

"Harper's dead," I heard him say. "Son of a bitch Eddie shot him…said it was an accident."

I always wondered if people instantly understood the consequences of words or moments that changed their lives forever, or if the reckoning crept upon them. For me, the weight of Cap's words was immediately apparent, pinning me to the ground. "You told me Eddie wasn't going to be there!" I hissed at him. "You said it was going to be you talking to Harper about restrictions."

"I said it would be me or Ed, and Ed told me he could handle it," said Cap. His voice had a higher pitch than normal, an unfiltered fear. "He called an audible at the last minute and brought Eddie, thinking he needed some muscle. Harper fought 'em and the gun went off...and the blood just kept coming. He's gone, man. This thing is totally fucked."

People were walking past the door shouting allegiance to their team, inhabitants of a different dimension than the conversation I found myself in. I forced myself to think clearly. "What if they just go to the police and say it was an accident?"

"They shot a guy in the neck and killed him," growled Cap, sounding more like himself already. "They're not going to turn themselves in for murder. Use your goddamned head. They took his car and drove out near Mitchell where no one would snoop around, and they got rid of the body."

"They buried it?"

"They burned it, along with Harper's car. I doubt that the police know anything at this point. Ed said he got rid of everything except..."

"Except what?"

"Except Harper's phone. It might have been left at the park."

"Are you fucking kidding me?" I shouted. "They're going to see phone calls and texts from me on there. They're going to figure out I was supposed to meet with him!"

"You're assuming they can get into his phone."

"They're going to get into his phone!" I screamed. "He's the mayor of Sioux Falls and your goons just fucking killed him. He's not some homeless guy. He's got a wife and daughter wondering where the hell he is. Hundreds of people work under him. Police are going to find out what happened to him and we're all going to go to jail."

"Hold on a minute," said Cap. "You and I didn't kill

anybody, so let's fucking relax. I'll talk to Ed and see if those guys can hide out for a while and keep their mouths shut. OK? Maybe it was a random act of violence and they never find out who did it. I mean, it's possible. The key right now is not to do anything stupid. Just watch the football game and try not to freak out, and let's get rid of these phones and say we lost 'em somewhere, if anyone asks."

Watching the game meant fighting off images of Harper's bloodied body, his torn-open neck and panicked eyes, knowing I set the nightmare in motion. Watching the game meant not reaching out immediately to police to facilitate the arrest of the scumbags who ambushed the mayor, murdered him and disposed of his body. That's what Cap meant by not doing something stupid. He meant steering clear of the right thing, avoiding it like the plague, shutting down the part of our makeup that separates us from animals and grasping at self-preservation, which is exactly what I did. By the time the teams took the field and I saw Nathan in his No. 80 jersey getting introduced with the starting offense, pumping his arms in the air, I figured that whatever was coming was going to happen anyway, and it could wait another two hours. Everything inside the dome – loudspeaker, drum line, crowd reactions, Connie's voice – reverberated in my skull, leaving my ears ringing. I forced myself to focus on elements of the action, defensive formations and play schemes, that I otherwise might have ignored, desperate to give my mind tasks to perform.

I started getting texts from Gina and Patrick early in the second half, after Catholic Central scored on a long pass play for a 10-0 lead. The mayor was missing, and sources said police suspected foul play. Something about blood being found, but no body. Could they go with anonymous sources or should they wait for something solid? "No anonymous sources," I texted back and then turned off my phone. I would need to find a way to get rid of it. There was sweat now trickling down my back, my heart racing. One of the biggest stories in Daily Gazette history was about to blow up and I was supposed to lead that coverage despite being an accomplice? It was Hollywood-level farce, unless you counted the charred body of a man who had trusted me and ended up dead. I knew that I would not be calling the shots at the Gazette much longer, certainly not after going radio silent at a time like this. I turned back to the game as Edison started moving the ball in the third quarter, with Brad Hawkins keeping the ball and plowing ahead for big gains, his body language all business. When the Nighthawks faced a third-and-goal from just inside the 10, Coach Talley reached deep in his playbook. Tommy Burgess took a handoff and ran right before wheeling around and firing a pass back to Hawkins, who had snuck down the left sideline and hauled in the throw to cut the lead to 10-7, sending the Edison sideline into hysterics. When Central fumbled the ensuing kickoff and Burgess barreled in for another score for a 14-10 lead, Connie jumped into my arms, squealing with delight.

My eyes were on not the touchdown celebration but the walkway behind the end zone, where a solitary security guard was now flanked by six police officers. It was a lot of security for a high school football game, but they appeared to be watching the action rather than scanning the crowd. When Catholic Central stormed downfield and scored on a pass to their tight end to take a 17-14 lead with three minutes left in the game, their grizzled old coach ran out to celebrate with his charges, one last triumph in sight. "I hate that guy," muttered Connie, as another parent shouted, "Plenty of time, Nighthawks! Let's go!" What followed was a season-defining Edison drive in which every yard mattered. Hawkins was limping now, battered by Central's defense but still fighting for daylight behind the blocking of Cale Schumacher, who showed signs of strain himself. The Nighthawks twice converted on fourth down, once on a quarterback sneak and the other on an option pitch to Burgess, who barely made the marker. They had only reached midfield by that point, and time was running out. When they faced another fourth-down situation at the Central 46-yard line, just 20 seconds remained and the Crusader fans were on their feet. The play looked like a bust at the beginning, with Hawkins confronted by a Central defender seconds after taking the snap. He did a spin move to evade that rush and scampered to his right, looking downfield for someone to throw to. Burgess had left the backfield and was streaking across the middle with his arm up, calling for the ball. Brad unleashed a rocket that glanced off Tommy's chest and sailed high in the air, way up over the field, with players from both sides oblivious of its path. I was probably the only one who saw Nathan tracking the ball, racing to get his body under the arc of its flight, reading it perfectly, then thrusting his hands out at the right moment to catch it and run, trailed by stunned defenders who didn't have the speed to make up the distance.

The words coming out of Connie's mouth were incomprehensible as Nathan darted into the end zone and held the ball aloft before being mobbed by teammates, including a relieved Tommy Burgess, whose bear hug lifted Nate off the ground. Coach Talley yanked off his headset and embraced his assistants before placing his hands on his knees and staring straight down, trying to process what happened. It was deafening within the dome, even at half-capacity, and I grabbed Connie's hand and took off running, determined to get us down to the field, to our son, before everything fell apart. The celebration down there was a tempest of sweat and glory, protocols be damned. Students hugging anyone they could find, players shouting to the heavens, cheerleaders in clingy clusters, weeping with joy. Masks appeared to be optional. When they handed Talley the trophy, he raised it over his head, arms fully extended, unleashing a roar that rippled through his team and up to the parents, and soon everyone was jumping in unison, chanting "Night...Hawks! Night...Hawks!" Talley passed the trophy to Brad Hawkins, whose eye black was smudged on his face, headband soaked in sweat. He was searching the stands with his eyes, probably looking for Cap, who I had not seen at the game. Nathan was on the edge of the celebration, being interviewed on live TV about his catch. I could see the nervous excitement on his face as he replayed the action. By the time he got to Connie and me, he had explained it every which way, so I just grabbed him and pulled him close and told him I loved him, allowing the sobs to convulse my body and not holding back, fearing the uncertainty of what might happen once I let go.

I saw the flashing lights as soon as we exited the dome. Nathan was taking the bus back to Sioux Falls, but Connie was at my side and remarked on the law enforcement presence, making a joke about police escorts. Four squad cars and an unmarked vehicle were lined up where the parking lot began, with officers scanning faces and motioning for people to move along. As we walked closer, a stocky guy in street clothes came up to me and flashed a badge. Two of the officers were close behind him.

"Special Agent Stoll with the Department of Criminal Investigation," he said to introduce himself. "You're wanted for questioning in a case involving Mayor Michael Harper."

"Can this wait until we get back to Sioux Falls?" I said. "Or can I maybe speak to you on the phone while my wife drives? My son just played in a football game..."

"Afraid not," he said. "I need you to come with me now."

I handed Connie the keys and told her to reach out to a lawyer we both knew, fending off her questions about what the hell was happening. I knew that saying anything, even to calm her fears, could be used against me, and I wanted to understand my options. Stoll put me in the back of his vehicle and told an officer to ride in the passenger seat, lights flashing to cut through traffic. The rain had picked up, distorting my view of the dome as we pulled away, a blurred canvas of colors and scattering crowds.

SEVENTEEN

My first impression of Graham Madsen was not as a lawyer. He graduated from Edison the same year as Connie, so I met him at their 20th reunion, where he regaled us at the hotel bar with stories of keg stands and Def Leppard sing-a-longs. I sized him up as one of those people who didn't long for the glory days because of diminished stature – he was a respected defense attorney in Sioux Falls – but because he was regarded as athletic and physically potent in high school, as opposed to his middle-aged incarnation of slight frame, dyed brown hair and darting eyes, keen to please behind tortoiseshell glasses. He achieved a measure of national renown by successfully defending a Chicago rapper busted at the Sioux Falls airport with marijuana edibles, exposing the deficiency of the state's draconian drug laws and getting him off with a suspended sentence, earning an Instagram shout-out and the appellation of "OG," which Graham was quick to tell us meant "original gangster," just like the high school days.

He found me in a back room at the campus police department, where Special Agent Stoll set up operations for the night. I was still in my Edison High apparel, feeling years removed from the exultation of Nathan's heroics, darkened by violent deeds. The question of whether my son would ever forgive me was excruciating to ask and impossible to answer, like so many other matters at hand. Graham got right down to business, telling me he had spoken with Stoll and his team, who were in touch with the state attorney general. His demeanor was markedly more formal than our earlier encounters and I considered the rather likely possibility that he had also been friendly with the mayor.

"The guys who did this, the guys who were there and pulled the trigger, are in an awful lot of trouble," said Graham, taking off his glasses and rubbing his eyes. "With elements of domestic terrorism and what looks like an orchestrated ambush and botched kidnapping, the death penalty could be in play. They're going to link you to some of these crimes because you were the one who set up the meeting. They can establish that from Harper's phone data, which is why you're here. Michael was the kind of guy who let his wife know his passcode." I was surprised that things were moving so quickly. Had Cap talked to the agents already? I had the impression that he was being held in the same building, engaged in separate conversations, and Graham must have sensed what I was thinking.

"The reason they picked up Mr. Hawkins and yourself at the football game was because of the urgency of the situation," he said. "They thought the mayor might still be alive, but now they know that's not the case." He paused for a moment, allowing for the possibility that I had not grasped that reality. "So we're talking first-degree murder, and they're weighing conspiracy charges as to your involvement. That would be bad, to put it in layman's terms."

It occurred to me that he had not yet asked me for my side of the story. Wasn't that what defense lawyers were supposed to do? He had his glasses back on and was staring at me with those beady eyes, trying to assess my level of culpability. If he was expecting me to just start shouting my innocence to the rooftops like in some shitty movie, he would be disappointed.

The silence became unbearable, so I said in a level voice, "I had no idea what those guys were going to do, Graham. I was coerced into setting up the meeting – they had some leverage on me – and they said they just wanted to persuade Harper to drop some of his Covid restrictions and allow the football game to go forward."

He adjusted his mask to cover his nose without losing eye contact. "Did you want the football game to go forward?"

"Of course," I said. "I was on public record saying that. That doesn't mean I wanted to kill somebody to make it happen. These guys used me to get access to Harper, and I foolishly went along without knowing how dangerous they were. Yes, I wanted my son to play in the state finals and I did some stupid shit, but I'm not a domestic terrorist. You know me better than that, right?"

He didn't answer, but it didn't matter. He was already negotiating a lesser charge based on cooperation, which meant I would tell them everything I knew. "You have no priors, and they would have a hard time convincing a jury that you thought that meeting would be anything more than a verbal exchange," he told me. "You're a longstanding member of the community with no real motive to harm the mayor. Still, you have some exposure here, and they want to poke around a bit. Just answer their questions, be careful with your words, and I'll step in if I need to. A lot depends on how much you give them. If you cooperate fully, I can maybe get this down to accessory, which is still a felony, but you'd be out in a couple of years."

By the time Stoll entered the room and collapsed into a chair, his adversarial instincts had been holstered. His caustic delivery, buttressed by jutted chin behind his mask, receded into a grudging familiarity now that we shared the goal of compiling evidence for a capital murder. I didn't bother to mention that I had written several editorials decrying South Dakota's recent use of the death penalty, figuring no one cared about me as a journalist anymore, least of all Stoll. One of the agents read me my rights as Graham took a seat beside me with a cup of coffee, glancing at his watch.

"Your counselor tells me that you had no idea these guys had violent intentions when you set up the rendezvous with Harper," said Stoll. "What did you think they intended to do?"

I told him about my conversations with Cap and Ed about Harper's ramped-up pandemic response and their vehement objections. The F.A.R. boys knew that I shared Cap's anger about school closures and what they would mean for Edison's championship hopes. Cap told me they wanted to have a discussion with the mayor about these issues, and they figured Harper would not agree if he knew it was them showing up.

"So you were angry at the mayor?" Stoll asked.

"He was concerned," Graham countered, shooting me a look. "At no time did my client expect or even wildly imagine that his valid concerns about policy would translate into violence on the part of people he barely knew."

Stoll sifted through his notes. "Did you not go pheasant hunting with Cap Hawkins? Did you not attend F.A.R. meetings at his shop? Did you not witness a member of the F.A.R. group trying to accost the mayor at a press event outside City Hall? For someone who's an outsider to this group, you sure hang around them a lot."

I glanced at Graham, who nodded for me to go ahead. "I met Cap Hawkins because our sons play for the same high school football team," I said, "which is why we were both at the dome tonight, as you know. I have no connection with Ed and Eddie and didn't plan to attend a F.A.R. gathering. I just happened to be there dropping my mower off and they started talking about Covid restrictions and lecturing me about some of the things I've written. I couldn't wait to get out of there, to be honest. Cap told me Ed had some involvement in protesting lockdowns in Michigan, and I later learned that Norah Newcombe, Governor Lawton's policy director, had spoken to militia groups awhile back, before the pandemic broke out."

Stoll glanced at the other agent as soon as I mentioned Newcombe, part of some understanding they had. He gestured at me to keep talking.

"It's hard to explain, but there was a lot of pressure building at the Gazette and with Cap and those guys, and I wanted my son's football game to happen. I don't deny that. But when I set up the meeting at the park, I thought it was going to be Cap showing up, not Ed and Eddie. I certainly didn't know they were going to bring a gun."

"Why didn't you just tell them no?" asked Stoll. "Why lie to Harper when you knew, at the very least, it was going to look bad for you professionally."

I asked to speak with Graham in private, telling him about my trip to Teasers and the compromising photo, wondering if I should disclose it all. He said that if anything, it helped my cause, showing Cap engaged in extortion and forced my hand. When I told him Cap might have put something in my drink that night, he waved me off, either because it wasn't relevant or he didn't believe me. So I laid out for Stoll the sordid details, or at least what I remembered. He listened intently and huddled with one of the other agents before returning to the table. I wondered what time it was, figuring that adrenaline was the only thing keeping me awake. Oddly enough, my head felt as clear as it had for several days.

"I'm in position to tell you that the guy you knew as Ed was not in fact Ed," Stoll said. "His name is William Hessman, and he was one of the men investigated for a plot to kidnap Michigan's governor over the summer, plans that were hatched during a rally at the state capitol. Among the actions discussed were apprehending the governor at her vacation home and using explosives to blow up a bridge to prevent law enforcement from responding. Hessman got off with a minor charge, as did his son, Billy, after their lawyer claimed they were just Trump supporters shooting their mouths off. They came to South Dakota to cool their heels but ended up getting fired up again, with Hawkins egging them on."

"Cap told me that Ed, or whatever his name is, is his ex-wife's brother," I said.

"That could be. We'll find out," Stoll said. "Most of what Hawkins told us has checked out, including information that led to Harper's body and car, as well as where the Hessmans have been staying in Sioux Falls. We arrested them in the parking lot without incident, unless you count the younger one crying like a baby."

As the conversation continued, I received almost as much information as I provided, a sign that they believed my story. To probe my recollections and gauge reaction, Stoll revealed in painstaking detail the events of that morning at Chatham Park and the chilling aftermath of the murder, reinforcing for everyone in the room the recklessness of my actions.

From what investigators were able to piece together, Harper got out of his vehicle and had reached the driver's side door of the Ford Escape before he realized it wasn't me. The Hessmans got out and told him they wanted to talk about calling off the mitigation measures and school closures. Harper said something like "this is bullshit" and turned to leave, at which point Billy pulled a handgun and told him to walk over to the picnic shelter. They told him to text his chief of staff that he wasn't feeling well and would be working from home, and that he had decided to think about school closures over the weekend and wouldn't make an announcement until Monday. According to what they told Hawkins, they demanded Harper's phone at that point and tossed it aside so he couldn't do anything funny with it. After some back and forth, they told him it was time to go for a ride. Harper refused.

"He knew getting into the car was a bad idea," said Stoll. "So he lunged at Billy, which the Hessmans will probably use for some ridiculous self-defense claim, and the gun went off. Harper was shot underneath the ear. They panicked and threw him in the trunk of the Audi, which William drove. Billy hopped in the Ford because they didn't want to leave it behind. They're in full freak-out mode now, and Harper doesn't last long before he dies, blood all over the trunk. So they call Hawkins, who curses their existence and tells them where to go to get rid of the body. He claims he only did this so he could tell authorities where to find them, but we're not so sure. Anyway, when Hawkins asked William where Harper's phone was, his response was, 'Oh shit.'"

The phone was discovered by a morning walker in the park, who also saw blood on the pavement nearby. She called the police, who took possession of the phone and secured the scene. Harper's wife was getting antsy because he hadn't responded to any of her calls or texts, which was unusual. When she called his office, they told her he had called in sick, which she knew wasn't true because she was at home.

"She called the police and a detective asked her if Harper would have any occasion to go to Chatham Park, just on a hunch," said Stoll. "They didn't mention the blood at that point. But she did call the phone when they asked her to and it rang right in front of them. After getting the passcode, they saw your phone call and Harper's text from the previous night. That's when things started to accelerate, and they called me."

They picked up Cap for questioning because he had made previous threats to City Hall and they had a file on him. He was spotted outside the dome before the game and apprehended after a brief scuffle. He said he would spill his guts if he could watch the second half, making sure to note that his son was Edison's star quarterback. "We told him he could and then changed our mind after he gave us what we wanted," said Stoll. "Life's a bitch, I guess."

Cap provided directions to an abandoned barn near his hometown, where agents found the charred chassis of the Audi and a body believed to be Harper's, burned beyond recognition. "We're waiting on dental records but we're 99.9 percent sure it's him," said Stoll. "The thing that bothers me is, if you say it's an accident, why not take him directly to a hospital, where they might have been able to save his life? Just drop him off at the ER and take off. Instead he died in the trunk of his own car, trapped and terrified and bleeding out. That's no fucking accident."

The clarity in my head wavered, replaced by familiar fog. I tried to picture Harper at the park, enraged at his assailants, confused by my absence, terrified at being shot, not ready to die. I thought of his wife and daughter, his stories of debate clashes and playground rivalries, his dream of running for governor. There had clearly been an agenda for him to meet with me in private, a way to curry favor and influence coverage. But those encounters opened a window into his personality that was otherwise shut tight, and I repaid him by sending mindless zealots his way at the break of dawn, almost like pulling a trigger. As Stoll gathered his papers and prepared to leave, he left no doubt that he agreed with that assessment.

"Don't think that you're some kind of hero for pouring your heart out and taking a deal," Stoll said. "That's not what happened here. Not by a long shot."

If Graham thought that comment was out of line, he didn't say so. He just pulled me aside for some parting words before heading out, and it struck me that I could not simply walk out the door with him and make my way home. I would need to get used to that, because I had decided not to accept bail even if it was offered. Freedom was not something I particularly deserved, not for a while.

"They'll keep you here tonight and take you to Sioux Falls tomorrow," Graham told me. "You'll be arraigned Monday, and the story will be all over the national news. I guess I don't need to tell you that. We'll plead guilty to accessory to a felony with the stipulation that you see daylight in three years or less, assuming you're a model inmate. That's a lot better than anyone else in this scenario is going to do."

He stopped at the door and thought for a minute before turning around. "When I talked to Connie on the way down here, she was pretty rattled," he said. "More information was coming out. She told me to tell you that she needs some time to think, and so does Nathan. Don't be surprised if you don't hear from them, at least for a few days. I think it's a fair request."

He signaled to the cop at the door that he was taking his leave before quickly poking his head back in. "Congratulations on the state championship," he said. "Go Nighthawks."

EIGHTEEN

The television in the dayroom of the Minnehaha County Jail switched to local news after "Judge Judy," eliciting groans from some inmates. Most of them ignored current events beyond the perceived injustice of their legal entanglements, ranging from meth possession to armed robbery in my unit of new arrivals. Due to Covid protocols, we were given cloth masks and kept apart from other inmate groups for a 14-day period, with a few hours outside our cells each day to make phone calls or take a shower. Watching the news offered grim reminders that life carried on without people like Joey Archambeau, a former high school distance runner from Eagle Butte charged with hit and run and resisting arrest. He insisted that I covered the state cross country meet in Huron his senior year, of which I have no recollection, and that he finished second after fading down the stretch, blaming it on the six pack he guzzled the night before. "The only news I care about I get from my family," Joey told me on our second day, hair slicked back from his shower. "I sure as hell don't care about the weather."

My situation was different, of course, and he knew it. The murder of Michael Harper, with its grisly particulars and political overtones, was the top trending story in America. Reporters from national outlets poured into Sioux Falls to shed light on how Trump-loving militia members ambushed and killed a progressive mayor over coronavirus restrictions, raising alarms about domestic terrorism. Kidnapping plots against Michigan's governor, dismissed by some as comically inept, took on greater significance as F.A.R.'s involvement in Harper's death became known. The fact that it happened in South Dakota, where Governor Lawton's hands-off pandemic approach frustrated public health experts while uniting Covid skeptics, created a perfect storm of ideological divide. "Heartland mayor tried to raise concerns about the virus – they killed him for it," read one of the cable TV chyrons, allowing the word "they" to cast a wide net. My involvement as a journalist added intrigue, but the fact that a Democratic mayor was targeted made it less appealing for "fake news" fanatics to attack mainstream media. The editor of South Dakota's largest newspaper helping to lay a trap that proved deadly for Sioux Falls' mayor was not viewed as an indictment of journalists in general, but rather a systemic failing within the workings of the Daily Gazette, the ramifications of which were not fully known.

I looked up to see Patty Harper, the widow, on TV with her daughter. They were standing on their front sidewalk, masked up, making an appearance likely negotiated to bring an end to reporters' encampment in front of their house. It was distressing to compare their comportment, strained from ultimately fruitless attempts to grasp the unfathomable, to that of election night, when the realized dreams of a husband

and father reflected on their faces. Harper's daughter was a recent college graduate with the same coppery brown hair as her mother. There were traces of Michael in her movements, such as how she instinctively reached out to comfort Patty as she began speaking, angling her head downward in a gesture of piety, or perhaps hiding her tears. I felt a catch in my throat that I repelled quickly, remembering where I was. One of the inmates was chirping loudly until someone told him to shut up so we could hear Patty as she addressed the media. "Michael would have wanted us to remain strong even as we confront the reality of life without him and the horrific actions that took him from us," she was saying. "But simply holding it together is not enough. As a family, we seek answers and justice for this despicable act. The idea that people in our midst could be so offended by safety measures for the good of this city that they would murder the man in charge of making such decisions makes us fear for our country's future. Michael wanted to bring people together. It's why he ran for mayor. 'It takes two flints to make a fire,' he'd say, trying to build connections. The notion that a supposedly respected citizen of Sioux Falls, a member of the media entrusted with informing the public, could help tear us apart makes it even harder to take. So we will stand strong, but we will not stand pat. We will demand appropriate punishment for those who have placed a senseless stain on this city." She ignored questions while putting her arm around her daughter and returning to the house, trailed by the trill of camera shutters. I disappointed myself by appraising not the sting of her words but the possibility that she might have a future in politics, musings that were interrupted by inmates raising a ruckus in my direction, emboldened by her judgment. Joey told them to relax, and then he grinned at me and said, "Of all the politicians out there, why did you have to kill the one guy that I liked?"

Truth be told, most of the inmates didn't treat me as a killer. As a mere accessory, I hadn't earned that level of respect. Some had read my columns in the Gazette and thought I could help them with their cases, as if I would set up shop and continue informing readers from my cell. Those days were over. I received my official notice of termination from the corporate office after pleading guilty at my arraignment, but I didn't share that with Joey and the rest of them. I didn't share much of anything, partly due to my darkened mood but also because Graham told me the less chatter the better, until my sentencing went through and I was transferred to the penitentiary. Even then, keeping quiet made sense. I would probably have to testify against Cap and the Hessmans, who were being held in a higher-security unit of the jail. William and Billy faced first-degree murder and kidnapping charges, while Cap was still in flux. His eagerness to strike a deal didn't negate the fact that he conspired not just in the ambush of Harper but the cover-up, despite helping police find the body. His role in founding F.A.R. and hounding Harper, not to mention grooming me as an accomplice, pointed to significant time behind bars. The thought of seeing him again, even in a court setting, turned my stomach. I thought of Brad and how the kid's triumphant moment, something he and his dad had envisioned since he first donned a helmet, was rendered meaningless so soon after being achieved, much like Nathan's miracle catch.

At least Nate still had Connie, and he hadn't devoted his entire life to the pursuit of athletic glory. He had a chance to get through this mess. Brad had no relationship with his mother, from what I'd been told, and was no stranger to trouble before any of this happened. His was just one of many lives that had been upended, a realization that made it easier for me to accept my punishment rather than railing against the system like those around me. I had my own cell and spent time reading whatever I could pluck from the cart, including a copy of *Hard Times* by Dickens, which suited my disposition. I watched the news when I could and took an occasional shower. Most of the guys left me alone, other than the time a guy busted for manslaughter muttered "Remove yourself, motherfucker" when I sat at his table in the dayroom, a request I was happy to grant.

I had daily access to the Gazette, where I learned that Harper's chief of staff was running things until he and the city council could figure out when and how to choose a new mayor. It had been so long since a top executive died in office that the city clerk had to go back through the charter to make sure they followed the rules. Lawton held a press conference and said all the right things, calling Harper's death "an unthinkable tragedy" and decrying the rise of "factions that work outside the boundaries of law and decency to achieve ignoble ends." But national outlets linked the governor to Trump in think-pieces detailing how dangerous rhetoric sparked extremist movements in a politically charged climate. Some drew parallels to the militia movements leading up to the Oklahoma City bombing of 1995, cautioning that more bloodshed could be on the way. Trump's refusal to concede the election, regaling his supporters with unfounded accusations of electoral abuses in battleground states won by Biden, added to an aura of unease.

Lawton had not only refused to distance herself from "rigged election" rhetoric but had fundraised off it, all while downplaying the Covid threat and attacking Democratic governors for pursuing mask mandates and other measures. The hope was that Harper's death would serve as a call to reason, if only that were possible. "Now that blood has been shed in the name of so-called freedom, perhaps it is time to give pause," a South Dakota Democratic legislator was quoted as saying in the Gazette. "This is the time for responsible leadership, not slings and arrows." The article euphemistically mentioned Norah Newcombe's "speaking engagements" with militia groups, adding that she was cooperating with the attorney general's office and taking a leave of absence, a consequence that seemed insufficiently severe. The same report, with Patrick's byline, described my involvement as an "unlikely alliance" with the F.A.R. group in which my relationship with Harper "was exploited to allow the ultimately deadly deception to occur." The front-page editorial they ran the next day was more direct, pointing out my guilty plea and noting that I was no longer affiliated with the newspaper or its parent company, language that Gina probably copied and pasted from the corporate office. "The Daily Gazette strives to report the news and not become the focus of it," the editorial continued. "The fact that a member of our leadership team egregiously violated these principles is unacceptable and not reflective of the values of our organization. We will work hard to regain your trust and maintain our mission at a time when local and independent news sources are as important as they've ever been."

My virtual visit with Connie was delayed for a few minutes by technical issues, and then suddenly she was on the screen.

I could tell exactly where she was in our house, sitting at the dining room table with her back to the kitchen, Lillie probably at her feet. It sounded like the refrigerator fan was acting up, a nuisance to which she had become numb. Her face was drawn but still alluring, the sort of gifted beauty that survives the ravages of sudden and unimaginable hardship, at least on the surface. This was the toughest test, but hardly the first. How many times had I taken her for granted, forcing her into a pantomime of happiness while disillusion hovered nearby? When we first dated, Connie complained that she frequently called me to hear my voice during the day, but I never did the same. Of course, it was not just about the phone call but whether I was thinking about her, whether I cared. Would it have pained me to reach out, even with nothing to say? The simplest of regrets are the hardest to bear, and now the tide had turned. She consented to this virtual visit because Graham urged her to, provided we didn't discuss details of the case, and it was probably a one-time thing. I tried to put myself in her place, seeing me in a black-and-white jumpsuit, shoulders bowed in a befouled cubicle, looking exactly on the surface as I felt inside, undeserving of her time and attention.

"How does this work?" she was asking. "Do I just start talking?"

"Yes…I wasn't sure the sound was on," I said. "How are you?"

"Well, let's see. How am I? That could take awhile. I ran into one of my best friends getting gas today and she pretended not to see me, just looked right through me before getting in her car and driving off. I was told to take two weeks off work for things to 'settle down,' as they put it, not for my mental well-being but because they're concerned about losing business. And Nathan didn't want to go to school today because he's getting bullied by people who want to know why his dad wanted the mayor dead, and that includes teachers. This is a kid who should have been greeted like a conquering hero after what he did in that game, and he doesn't want to even show up. That about sums up how I'm doing."

Her thoughts crystallized when she was angry, a rhetorical anomaly that allowed her to get me on the defensive. "I can't talk much about the case," I told her, "but I hope you know that what those people are saying is not right. I never wanted anyone to die."

"You really think people are making that distinction?" she said. "You give them too much credit. You pleaded guilty. You're going to prison. You lost your job. You consorted with people who you wouldn't normally give the time of day, doing all this crazy shit behind my back, and for what? A football game? Seriously? Do you expect your son to thank you for your service?"

It was heartbreaking to picture Nathan being bullied at school, so I pushed it out of my mind. The surge of acceptance he'd experienced after last summer's football overtures was an illusion that he and I embraced, wanting it to be real. Now even his game-winning catch seemed like a trick of the light. I asked Connie if I could speak with him and she said he wasn't home. She had always been a bad liar. "Nate needs time to figure things out, and so do I," she said. "I've got reporters knocking at the door, both your parents have been calling me constantly, and I'm trying to figure out when and if I can go back to work. If I lose my job, we're going to be a no-income household. Not sure if you've thought about that or not."

I didn't answer right away. I was thinking back to our

wedding night, hours after the reception, when she asked me to usher people out of our hotel suite but I persuaded her to keep the party going, and we ended up passing out in our clothes on opposite ends of the bed, oblivious of finally being alone. Connie had packed a silk negligee that her mother had gotten her that she planned to wear, and it bothered her that the imagined scenario for consummating our marriage – though we had lived together for almost a year – had been displaced by peals of laughter and awkward embraces from people we barely knew. She had an idea of how our story should go. Recklessness was not part of the plan. Her husband, the eventual father of her son, was supposed to be stable and supportive, like the guy who didn't allow his son to play with toy guns and hovered over him at every moment growing up. She had missed the signs of slippage, the easing of standards, and now here I was sitting in jail after allowing myself to be manipulated by some of the most reckless people I'd ever met. The biggest difference was that Connie still loved me after the wedding-night debauchery, after years of one-sided affection in our marriage, of thinking mainly of myself and my own intentions, and this time I wasn't so sure. She said something like "I can't hear you" or "I can't do this" and then her face was gone, just as suddenly as it had appeared, back to the life I was no longer a part of, the one I had failed to protect.

———

I passed Joey sitting and watching TV on the way back to my cell. "What's good?" he said, his usual greeting, but I didn't feel like talking. That must have bothered him, because he made fun of me sulking and loudly surmised that my visit had not gone well. "Trouble in paradise, folks!" he said with a grin, looking around to see if he got a reaction. When I kept walking, I heard him say to one of the other inmates, "Actions have consequences, man. I don't care if you're an old white dude or not. Actions have consequences!" He raised his voice and drew out those last words to make sure I heard him. "Story of my life, bro," the other guy said. When I got to my cell, I lay down and grabbed the copy of *Hard Times*, a weathered paperback with a portrait of a young girl on the cover, a spinner from a textile mill, her searching eyes and interlaced hands delicate for the work she performed. Despite my surroundings, it felt satisfying to immerse myself in the pages of a book rather than scrolling through my phone, seeking the next object of outrage or titillation. It reminded me of my college days, lying in bed at my off-campus house, reading a novel a night for literature class, falling in love with language.

Reading had made me a better writer, and there was much more to learn. When I got to the part where the laborer Blackpool ponders his love for poor factory girl Rachael, I recalled it as a passage I highlighted and read in class as an example of writing that stirred my soul, precisely what the professor asked us to consider. The fact that it had the same effect so many years later, the words blurring as I read them, said something about the resiliency of human nature, no matter how torn and frayed. "The wind blew from the quarter where the day would soon appear, and still blew strongly," Dickens wrote. "It had cleared the sky before it, and the rain had spent itself or travelled elsewhere, and the stars were bright. He stood bareheaded in the road, watching her quick disappearance. As the shining stars were to the heavy candle in the window, so was Rachael, in the rugged fancy of this man, to the common experiences of his life."

NINETEEN

In the spring of 2020, as coronavirus loomed as a sinister and insoluble equation, a city worker approached me in our driveway. He was inspecting trees in the neighborhood, seeing which ones required trimming, and wanted to discuss branches from our elms that dangled over the road. The guidance was still muddled on masks; neither of us wore one. Clad in work vest and helmet, the man walked toward me until I abruptly raised my palms outward, stepping back and sputtering "no, no, no" to stop his advance. He pulled up sheepishly, keeping his distance for the conversation that followed, talking loudly over the roar of chain saws down the block. I felt silly after that exchange, treating a tree trimmer as if he were an approaching predator, but we were learning the nature and severity of threats and constantly asking questions. Who and what could hurt us? How might we protect ourselves? Is it safe to interact? I used similar caution with the correspondence I received after being transferred to the state penitentiary to serve out my sentence. Letters arrived daily, especially at the beginning, from not only friends and acquaintances, but national media, religious organizations, documentary filmmakers, legal advocates, and political extremists from both sides. I assessed the threat level of each situation, as the virus and my association with Cap Hawkins had taught me, trying to discern if they were on my side or working an angle, seeking low-rent residuals where infamy resides.

Like a true journalist, Gina had relinquished the rudiments of handwriting, sending a printed-out Word document to address my downfall. She explained the thinking behind the front-page editorial and noted that much of the language had been dictated from corporate, as I suspected. With that out of the way, she proceeded to explain how her opinion of me as a journalist and mentor had been shattered by the events surrounding Harper's death. "I will never forget that night," she wrote. "It was one of those breaking news stories that defines a career, and we needed your leadership and insight. We were wild-eyed with reports coming in, trying to separate rumor from fact, and we could not reach you. Then to discover that you had not only abandoned the Gazette but betrayed everyone around you and contributed to the plot against the mayor – it's hard to find words for that." She compared it to a female volleyball coach in high school who helped her find confidence as a player, working after practice on serves and attacks at the net, and then one day was gone when inappropriate relationships with past students came to light. "One thing I've learned is that role models, or people's assumptions about them, are fragile," she wrote. "It's tough to put them back together after they break." My fall from grace contributed not just to Gina's disillusionment but the institutional struggles of the Gazette. Two reporters had quit amid the firestorm of controversy following my arrest, and Gina said she was considering leaving as well. Advertising revenue, already ravaged by the pandemic, was sinking to dangerous depths, meaning Eugene White's pronouncement after the 1953 fire that the rebuilt newspaper could withstand the onslaught of a plague had been overly optimistic.

My mother wrote to tell me that Wayne quarantined for 14 days so he could travel to stay with her and her husband in Michigan after news broke of my dangerous behavior, as she put it. Sitting around the kitchen table at night, they contemplated warning signs that could explain why I would throw away my career and family with such callous disregard. She mentioned the divorce and how it was harder on me than Wayne, at least outwardly so, pointing to my ill-fated alliance with the Vickers boys and the run-in with police. She said she had tried to keep her friends from finding out about my involvement in Harper's murder but found it impossible due to the amount of national coverage. That was the hardest part of the letter for me, imagining my mom trying to strike my sins from public record, like the bathrobe-clad woman in a movie I saw who snatched newspapers off every doorstep in her neighborhood due to harmful headlines, ultimately breaking down at the futility of the task. There is no doubt that my mom was proud to see me get my college degree, find success in far-off South Dakota and grace her with a grandson, and for a long time those nods to respectability outweighed concern for my emotional well-being. "I always wanted to believe the best and had many occasions to do so," she wrote. "I fear that with those positive elements in your life extinguished, you'll struggle to find your way when they finally let you go." She signed off by expressing her love for

me, a sentiment shaded by the understanding that my transgressions were inconvenient for her, and true forgiveness
would come slowly.

She had a more fluid writing style than my father, whose
letter seemed hastily crafted, armed with political animus.
"Those guys you got mixed up with were bad news – that's
obvious," he wrote. "But that doesn't mean the government
actions that pushed them over the edge were constitutional,
and now Biden wants it to last forever. Time for people to stop
living in fear." It was an odd takeaway after the murder of a
politician by domestic extremists, but he rarely considered
how such bombast sounded outside his ideological bubble. I
suspected that Covid had made his existence with Cynthia
on that South Carolina estate more insular, allowing ideas to
germinate in a fertile habitat, safe from logic or reason. He
asked about prison conditions, how they were treating me,
and then surprised me by saying he might come for a visit, a
gesture he had not made during the 16 years of his grandson's
existence. "I wouldn't mind talking to your lawyer about
grounds for early dismissal," he wrote, as if a retired advertising executive would bring legal strategies to light. "Three
years seems like a stiff sentence for something you didn't
really do." The opposite pull of my parents, one wondering
if I could atone for my transgressions and the other calling
for the release of an innocent man, suggested that salvation
existed somewhere in the middle, amid the fears and motivations of a restless mind, right where the trouble began.

I followed the news closely enough to know that William
and Billy Hessman were awaiting trial, their lawyers trying
various motions to move the proceedings out of Sioux Falls.
There was also a mental competency hearing pending for

Billy, probably an early salvo in his bid to fight off the death penalty. South Dakota's F.A.R. chapter had disbanded, and militia groups in Michigan and elsewhere weren't rushing to defend the Hessmans, whose murderous acts tarnished the anti-lockdown movement. As for Cap Hawkins, my cellmate heard he was hospitalized after trying to hang himself with a jail-issued face mask, an attempt foiled when a guard saw the cell window covered with toilet paper and figured something was up. The rumors were confirmed a few days later in the Gazette, which reported Cap would be placed in a suicide-resistant room at the jail, with no protrusions for him to hang himself and nothing but time to consider the life sentence he faced. "Son of a bitch is lucky to be alive," my cellmate said after I read him the article. "Or unlucky, I guess."

It wasn't long before Harper's death was replaced on front pages by the siege on the U.S. Capitol, occurring the same day as a pro-Trump rally in Washington and the counting of electoral votes in Congress. The far right's introspection following the tragedy in South Dakota was cast aside as militia groups found a new rallying cry, that of trying to prevent Biden from taking office, which he did a few weeks later, shielded by the National Guard. Political divisions that intensified with Trump in office and reached new intensity during the Covid crisis now focused on the fundamental ability of America to hold free and fair elections. The quest to restore normalcy transcended the pandemic, in other words, but no one was quite sure what normal represented anymore, or if it was worth seeking. These were notions I would have explored in editorials in my previous life, but now I ponder them while lying on my bunk, eyes on the ceiling, books and papers by my side. I am most restless at night, kept awake

by coughs and clamor, the drone of my roommate's snoring.
I try to put myself in Cap's place, the specter of never getting
out, wondering if I would go to the lengths he did to make the
guilt and loathing disappear. He was a coward, I told myself,
who stoked fear in others to obscure his own sense of dread.
I felt bad for his son, but Cap could go to hell.

I haven't responded individually to those who wrote letters.
I'm not ready for that. These thoughts I set free each day,
my personal Covid Chronicles, are an open letter to everyone
with mouths agape at my demise. The words aren't intended
to justify my actions but to explain how I ended up here, in
a place I used to visit with trepidation as a journalist, when
I knew I was welcome to leave. Fear and resignation thrive
here, but I stand strong. Following the example of Henry
Eagle Bull, I plan to teach writing to other inmates, helping
them with correspondence and amplifying their voice. The
scratching of pencil on paper soothes me as I look ahead to
days and weeks and months to come. I wonder when this all
ends and we take stock of ourselves, like refugees from a vast
war, how my words will be received by those I have failed.
Does understanding lead to forgiveness, or do fragments of
betrayal linger, keeping normal beyond our grasp? I pour
out my words and await their response, a child on the street
corner, watching the cars, searching in vain for the right one,
then beginning the long walk home.

ACKNOWLEDGEMENTS

Sincere appreciation to Asya Blue for her design work and patience with this project. Thanks also to Ron Hoffman for exhaustive editing and Emily Whitney for helping the story reach a wider audience. Furthermore, to all the reporters and editors I've worked with over the years, your commitment to enriching the community with quality journalism remains inspiring.

Made in the USA
Monee, IL
01 July 2022

98925881R00135